Boun

...very intense and hot... Those that love BDSM stories will want to add this one to the bookshelf. ~ *Literary Nymphs Reviews*

Got to love Sierra Cartwright and her decadent tales of love and lust!... This one's a keeper, so if a little BDSM and three-way action by the mighty pen of Ms Cartwright sounds good to you too, then don't miss Bound and Determined.
~ *Whipped Cream Reviews*

Total-E-Bound Publishing books by Sierra Cartwright:

Signed, Sealed & Delivered
Bound and Determined

Naughty Nibbles:
This Time
Fed Up

Bound Brits:
S&M 101

Night of the Senses:
Voyeur

Halloween Heartthrobs:
Walk on the Wild Side

Homecoming:
Unbound Surrender

BOUND AND DETERMINED

SIERRA CARTWRIGHT

Bound and Determined
ISBN # 978-0-85715-733-1
©Copyright Sierra Cartwright 2011
Cover Art by Posh Gosh ©Copyright 2011
Interior text design by Janet Marshall
Total-E-Bound Publishing

Published in 2011 by Total-E-Bound Publishing, Think Tank, Ruston Way, Lincoln, LN6 7FL, United Kingdom.

Total-E-Bound Publishing is an imprint of Total-E-Ntwined Limited.

Manufactured in the USA.

BOUND AND DETERMINED

Dedication

For BAB, lover of all things ménage!

Chapter One

Bollocks.

Jack Quinn propped his elbow on the polished wood bar of the lower downtown pub and drank deeply from the pint of stout as he watched the petite and smoking hot Sinead O'Malley move into action for a solo.

He'd seen pictures of her—his sworn enemy—online. His luggage contained a folder full of information about her.

He'd chased her across two continents and through half a dozen cities in the United States. He thought he knew everything about her yet nothing had prepared him for the first in-person sight of her.

He'd known she was an Irish step dancer, but the dossier provided by his grandmother's people hadn't mentioned that the talented Ms O'Malley also played three different types of drums as well as the bagpipes.

Seeing a good-looking woman, enemy or not, in snapshots was one thing, but he'd had no idea he'd have such an immediate, raw, unwanted masculine reaction to seeing her athletic body.

Her cutoff white T-shirt was too tight across the swell of her breasts and left part of her toned midriff bare. If she was wearing a bra, it wasn't very serviceable. He imagined he could see her nipples all the way from here.

Her kilt was way too fecking short. It barely covered her well-shaped arse. And when she danced he saw a pair of sexy black knickers. At least she wasn't commando beneath the skirt.

Her muscular legs were bare, and her socks had pooled around her ankles.

Even though he watched her squeeze the pipes from halfway across the pub, his cock hardened.

Noise in the room diminished as gazes turned towards the stage. Every man in the place was likely sporting an erection. Lust was palpable. If she were his woman, he wouldn't stand for her being dressed that way in public and he'd want her wearing a whole lot less in private.

He took another long drink from the glass. He'd be needing another pint in only minutes. A man needed fortification to manage the likes of Sinead O'Malley and manage her he would.

He wouldn't be leaving Denver without her in tow. He intended to possess her. Ride her. Claim her. Dominate her. Make her his submissive. Claim her as his.

The eight-hundred-year feud between their clans ended now even if he had to tie her to his bed and spank the sass out of her.

Since it wouldn't be seemly to drag her off the stage, bend her over, yank down her knickers, make her call him Sir as he fucked her ragged on top of a table, he bided his time.

She'd started dancing with the group a few years ago as a way to pick up a little extra cash. He hadn't taken the time to listen to the CD provided of her music and he was surprised by how much he enjoyed the sound of the Celtic-infused rock band that pulled from all nations. Or maybe he was just intrigued by the lass and wasn't really hearing the music.

All the other band members fell silent as she worked the pipes.

A spotlight hit her. He recognised the Kelly tartan...from her mother's side of the family. The Kellys were one of the few Irish clans entitled to wear a tartan—the same as the royal house of Stewart.

Because of the distance and the way she held the bagpipes, he couldn't quite read the writing on her white T-shirt. The distance and dim lighting made it impossible to see her eyes, even though the information he had on her said they were green.

Then again, the file said she had blonde hair. It hadn't mentioned the fiery highlights that seemed to ignite in the overhead lighting. It hadn't mentioned that the lengths fell in bedroom-like disarray across her forehead and around her face and shoulders.

It looked the way it might after a good, long, hard screw.

"Got your eye on that one, have you, mate?" the barkeep asked, pocketing the tip Jack had left on the bar. "She's been in here half a dozen times in the past year. A right handful, she is. Won't be having none of the likes of you." He glanced at her then back at Jack. "She won't be having any of us for that matter."

"We'll be seeing about that."

"Good luck. She vanishes after the show. She doesn't stay at the same place the rest of the band does. She's talented all right. But she ain't interested in any socialising. She'll cut any man to the quick."

Jack nodded, considering himself warned. "Fetch me another pint, mate."

The bartender nodded and moved off.

Jack returned to watching the woman. It could be worse, he supposed. She was passionate, if her music was anything to go by. In need of taming, if the bartender's words were anything to go by.

Her passion turned him on.

He'd want Sinead, no matter what his *máthair Chríona*, grandmother, said. The way Sinead moved her hips made his cock harden. He could almost imagine the way she smelt, of musk and desire.

He joined the applause as she ended her solo and she moved to the back of the stage.

He drank his second stout and enjoyed the rest of the set. Part of him wished she would dance again. Another part of him was relieved she hadn't. He wasn't sure his libido could take seeing her underwear and bare midriff.

At the end of the set, the gathered crowd gave a lukewarm applause. He watched Sinead place the pipes on the wooden planks, then plop herself down on an amplifier.

Her skirt rode even higher and she didn't sit like a lady. Now he knew why Yanks drank their beer so damn cold. 'Twas to cool the flames of ardour.

He watched — or more like it, stared — as she uncapped a bottle of water, tipped her head back and drank deeply.

The band's lead singer said a few words to Sinead then nodded and moved off, leaving her alone.

Jack seized the opportunity.

In a few steps, he was on the stage. A couple more brought them face-to-face, or, in this case, her face to his crotch. And wasn't this his lucky day? It wouldn't be long before he'd have her on her knees, hands secured behind her back as she sucked his cock. "Great show."

She smiled. It wasn't a warm and welcoming smile. It was more the smile of a princess. It was polite enough, dutiful, but it sure as hell wasn't inviting.

The houselights came up a little more.

This close to her, he saw a few beads of sweat on her brow and across the sweet curve of her upper lip. And he was also close enough to read the writing on her in-your-face T-shirt: *You're not rich enough. Smart enough. Or man enough. Don't even try.*

They'd be seeing about that, as well. "Do you intimidate most men, Sinead?"

"All men," she corrected, recapping her water bottle. "I don't have time for men." She levelled a gaze at him. "Even if I wanted a quick toss, it wouldn't be with an anonymous man. You groupies are all the same."

The way she talked about sex, with her brogue and feminine sensuality that nothing could disguise, made his cock throb. He wasn't just hard now. Not at all. He was ready. "Although I wouldn't mind bedding you, I'm not interested in a quick toss, Ms O'Malley."

"An autograph? Do you have a pen? Then perhaps you'll leave me the hell alone?"

Polite, wasn't she? "I'm not looking for an autograph."

"Well, then, if you'll excuse me?"

She stood and turned away. By the time she'd taken two steps, he'd curved his hand around her shoulder and applied enough pressure that she stopped.

Slowly she turned back to face him again. Since he stood nearly a foot taller than her, she had to tip her head back in order to meet his gaze. "Take your hand off me. I've another set to prepare for."

"I've travelled halfway round the world to meet you."

"You should have bought the CD and saved yourself several hundred pounds." Her smile was chilling. "You've met me." She reached her hand up to pry his fingers off her shoulder. "Release me immediately."

He was aware of the way she felt beneath him, womanly, but with unaccountable strength. He wanted her. "We've important things to discuss, Sinead O'Malley."

"You are beginning to annoy me." She exhaled. "I'm thinking maybe you're a bit off your rocker, Mr…"

He slowly released her.

"Jack." He extended a hand. She ignored it. *Smart lass.* "Jack Quinn."

"Jack Quinn?" Her mouth dropped.

A very perfect, very pink tongue sneaked out. Good God, didn't that cause another fantasy?

"*The* Jack Quinn? Hated enemy. Mad as a hatter?"

He didn't quite know what to say to that. A man who chased a woman halfway around the world because of a comb didn't seem to be all there.

"Sorry, I didn't recognise you without the horns and tail."

"I've never been the devil, Sinead."

"Couldn't prove that by my family."

She took her time looking him over from his head to his dusty shoes. Judging by her sneer, she found him wanting.

Not the usual reaction from the ladies.

"So you're the bastard who's been stalking me?"

"I've been trying to get an audience with your highness for a while now," he agreed.

"You've been following me for six thousand miles, Mr Quinn."

E-mails, letters, phone calls, messages at venues along the way. "You're a difficult woman to reach."

"I'm sorry to say you travelled all this way to have me reject you and your ridiculous marriage proposal in person." She moved an electrical cord out of the way with her toes. "Since you're apparently thick or stubborn or both, the answer to your proposal, Mr Quinn, is not just *no*. It's *hell no*. I don't care if it would make your grandmother happy or secure your family line. I will not marry you. Not now, not ever."

She gave him a sunny smile that really, he knew, meant 'fuck you'.

"You are blunt."

"I need to be as you're apparently addled. Now I'll thank you to get the hell off the stage and out of my life."

"We need to talk, Sinead. We *will* talk."

"I have nothing beyond that one word to say to you." She pulled back her shoulders. "I'm not interested in your family's problems."

Her green eyes flashed irritation and her voice dropped an octave or two. "I'm not interested in *you*, Jack Quinn."

She'd added the last, he supposed, in case he'd missed her point.

"You can get back on a plane and go home. County Mayo, isn't it?"

As if she had to ask. Their shared history went back well over eight hundred years. The details of the sordid events were recorded for all time in the *Annals of the Four*

Masters—the compilation of Irish history that dated back nearly two thousand years.

Sinead looked at him. Her eyes flashed venom. "*Cuimhnich air na daoine o'n d'thainig thu.*"

She speaks the tongue, does she? "Remember the men from whom you are sprung," he translated.

"I, for one, will never forget."

"It's not just my problem, Ms O'Malley. It's ours."

"Ours," she repeated. "Ours?" Her laugh was more an unladylike snort.

"Everything okay here, Sinead?" the drummer asked, climbing onto the stage and offering her a short glass of amber liquid. Good Irish whisky, Jack presumed.

"I can handle Mr Quinn myself." Sinead accepted the glass.

The young man glared at Jack when Jack unashamedly drank his fill of the woman in front of him. Did the whelp have a crush on the woman? Jaysus, were they screwing each other?

And too bad if they were.

Sinead was going to be his. He'd not let a gobshite stand in the way.

She tipped back her head, exposing the vulnerable column of her throat, then closed her eyes and downed the beverage in a single swallow.

She made a soft kissing sound as she closed her eyes in apparent rapture.

Lord have mercy.

He ached to stroke his knuckles along the curve of her cheekbone, trail the pad of his index finger down her nape...

She sighed. When she opened her eyes, she asked, "You're not just a bad dream? More's the pity." She smiled at her protector. "Mr Quinn was just leaving, Brandon."

"Bugger all," Jack said. "You might as well hear me out."

"You've nothing to say that I want to hear."

"Nothing?"

"Nothing except goodbye." She slid the glass onto the speaker.

"Ouch." He gave her his quick, calculated, disarming grin that always scored points in contract negotiations. It didn't seem to soften her at all.

"You sure you don't need help taking out the rubbish?" Brandon asked.

"Go on with you. If he hasn't left within a couple of minutes, I'll call security."

Jack wondered if she'd be so blasé if she knew he intended to tie her up, tie her down, drag her back to Ireland and his family home within the next twelve hours. Kicking, screaming, biting, it didn't matter. In fact, he looked forward to her fighting him. It would make his victory all the sweeter.

"Go," she told Brandon again.

The overconfident pup looked over his shoulder and glared at Jack before moving off.

"The lad, Brandon. Is he a member of your fan club?"

"One of the hundreds." She checked her watch, a whimsical piece with white gloves at the end of the hour and minute hands. "I'll give you two minutes." She folded her arms, with her left wrist on top, where she could keep an eye on the ticking seconds.

"Do you believe in curses, Ms O'Malley?"

"Not on your life."

She twitched. It was subtle, but her nose wrinkled and her brows furrowed. Being a descendent of the Kellys and O'Malleys, there was no way she didn't believe in curses.

"Or the Banshee?" According to Celtic legend, the Banshee was either human, fae, or even spirit. To some she was young and beautiful, to others, an old hag. She wailed, keened, cried, or dropped a comb as a portend of death or destruction.

"I believe in stuff you can touch with your hands, Mr Quinn. Instruments, balance sheets, ledgers. I don't have time to be fanciful."

He reached into his back pocket and pulled out a metal comb.

As the silver winked, reflecting the overhead lights, colour drained from her cheeks. He watched her fight the urge to take it from his hand, to see if it was real.

She had the same reaction his grandmother had.

"My *máthair Chríona* found this."

Instead of taking the comb, she reached for her whisky glass. Realising it was empty, she rolled the glass between her palms. "My condolences, in advance, to your family."

Bitch. Temper and temptation warred within him. No one mattered more to him than his *máthair Chríona*. His jaw tightened. The less civilised side of his nature demanded he sling Sinead over his shoulder, drag her from the room then find the nearest wall and slam her up against it.

He deliberately put the comb back in his pocket, his actions controlled. Then, anger in check, he discarded the option of fucking her ragged and settled for capturing her chin, not at all gently, between his thumb and forefinger. When he spoke, his tone was harsh, his words blunt. "You deserve a good hiding, Sinead."

That shut her up.

Heat chased up her cheeks, replacing the colour that had momentarily drained away when she had seen the comb. When she opened her mouth again, she was back in full form. "A good hiding, is it? I've already said you're not man enough for me."

"Shall we see?" He stroked his middle finger across the top of her lip. "I think I'm just the man to teach you to mind your manners, lass."

"You won't be touching me again, *diabhal.*"

Like *hell* he wouldn't. He intended to be on her. In her. "You are aware, wombat, that the Banshee doesn't follow all families. She does not follow the Quinns." He smiled viciously. "She follows the O'Malleys. My *máthair Chríona* believes the warning was meant for you."

The flush on her cheeks darkened.

With precise aim, firing back at the direct hit she'd scored, he added, "Not many of you left now, are there?"

"You really are a bastard, Quinn."

She curled her hand into a fist and Jack wasn't sure whether or not she was going to take a swing at him. Part of him hoped she did. Then he'd have every reason to sling her over his shoulder and drag her back to his hotel.

"*Go n-ithe an cat thú is go n-ithe an diabhal an cat.*"

May the cat eat you, and may the cat be eaten by the devil. Or her figurative meaning, *screw you.*

She trembled, though, despite her bravado, despite her hard words. He'd unnerved her. And, he wondered, what bothered her most—him, or the Banshee? "The curse ends with us, Sinead. With you becoming my bride."

She laughed. Really laughed. "You really are mad as a hatter."

Band members began moving towards the stage. The electric guitarist tuned his instrument, all but drowning their conversation.

Sinead unclenched her fist then clamped her hand on his wrist. "Your two minutes are up, Quinn bastard. I never want to see you again."

"Perhaps you didn't hear me. I'll be here when you've finished."

"I've no use for you, sir."

Was that the slight dig of her fingernails in his skin?

"Go home."

"Aye. And when I do, you'll be by my side. Mark my words, Sinead. You'll be Mrs Quinn."

"When my ancestors roll in their graves."

Her fingernails sliced into his skin. The woman had claws.

"This is no longer about you and me, lass."

"Sinead!" Brandon called.

"I've finished with you." She pulled her hand off his wrist.

She flipped her hair over her shoulder as she moved away, defiant and delicious.

He moved back to the bar.

"This one's on the house." The bartender slid a complimentary pint in Jack's direction. "I told you she was a tough one."

Jack looked at his wrist and studied the half crescents carved into his skin by his fiery opponent. "You warned me."

"She's only been here a few times, but we already call her the Titanic." The man swiped a white towel across the shiny wood. "Men see her lovely smile and think they're in for smooth sailing. Then afore you know it, you hit the ice — the ice in her veins."

Jack hoisted his glass in her direction.

Round one to the lovely lass from Westport.

Chapter Two

Sinead kept her gaze on Jack Quinn throughout the set.

Despite her blasé attitude, the damned comb and the man himself both unnerved her. It took all her concentration to remain focussed on the music.

She wanted to call Westport and check on her family. She wasn't as fanciful as the rest of her family, but the fact his *máthair Chríona* has supposedly found a comb bothered her. According to legend, he was correct. The Banshee followed the O'Malleys, not the Quinns.

He could be lying. Or his grandmother could have dropped the comb herself.

But there'd been something familiar in the design.

She'd seen a comb like that before, in her own *máthair Chríona's* home, shortly before the death of one of her aunts. She'd been a child, and after that, her grandmother had banned all combs from the house. No one, including Sinead, believed that getting rid of a comb could stop fate, could stop the Banshee.

She hadn't seen his comb clearly enough to be sure the etching was the O'Malley crest, but damn it, it could be.

No matter what she'd said to Quinn, she was unsettled.

She passed up the opportunity for the scheduled snare drum solo and remained at the back of the stage. She wanted to remain hidden from his prying eyes—even though the colour was a startling, inviting blue. Hiding from him was difficult, though. Jack watched her as intently as she watched him.

Ever since she'd been a little girl, she'd heard stories of the hated Quinns. According to the *Annals of the Four Masters*, a Quinn had kidnapped an O'Malley woman almost a thousand years ago, beginning a long feud that resulted in bloodshed.

The O'Malley family Bible had a drawing of a frightful devil, thin and red with a forked snakelike tail. She remembered crawling onto her great-grandmother's lap to look at the ancient pages. The woman had pointed to the picture and whispered, "That's what the Quinn men look like."

Sinead had outgrown her fanciful notions, or at least she'd thought she had.

When Jack had started trying to contact her, she'd imagined him as an odious little gnome, squat and balding. For good measure, she'd thought he might have a pair of spectacles resting at the end of a misshapen nose.

But in truth, the reality was much, much more disturbing.

Jack Quinn was tall and broad. His hair was dark, and perhaps a bit too rakishly long. Those piercing eyes seemed to see straight through any lie or subterfuge.

A hint of darkness shadowed his jaw. And if he'd been telling the truth, he'd been too busy chasing her across the world to stop for a shave.

He was muscular and tough, as she'd discovered when she'd dug her fingernails into his wrist. A lesser man would have objected or at least winced. Not Jack Quinn.

It had been his scent, though, that had really got to her. He smelt fresh and crisp, like the untamed wild coast of home.

He was everything she desired in a man and her damp knickers were proof of that.

Why, why, why did her body have to betray her? Why did she have to have such a feminine reaction to him? And when he'd threatened to give her a good hiding, she'd frozen on the spot. She hadn't doubted for a moment that he was serious and a searing white flash of desire had raced through her as she'd pictured herself upended over his knee.

She'd always dreamt of being with a man who was masculine enough for her. The men she knew were... She missed a beat on the snare drum... Brandon turned and looked at her quizzically. She nodded and found her rhythm again.

Most of the men she'd been with had been boring. There'd been one man in her past who had introduced her to the darker delights of sex. She'd had enough of a taste to whet her appetite. But she'd learned most men had no interest in the same things she wanted. Their idea of a spanking was a gentle tap. As if that would get her anywhere.

But in this man, Jack Quinn, hated enemy with his promises of a good hiding, a man willing to chase her halfway around the world, she might have met her match. The idea scared her as much as it fascinated her.

She noticed that the barkeep was speaking to Jack. Seizing the opportunity, she signalled to Brandon. She twisted her lips and pointed to her stomach, pretending to be ill.

When he responded by nodding, she put down her drum, snatched up her handbag that was the size of a small piece of luggage, and made a mad dash towards the toilets. She stayed inside for only a few moments then joined a group of laughing women who were leaving together. She was grateful women often travelled to the loo in small herds.

As short as she was, she didn't stand out among the women. She glanced over at the bar to make sure Jack was still occupied then she ran for the kitchen. She got several strange glances from the chefs, but she waved and called out, "I have a crazy fan after me. Don't tell him I came this way!"

One of the men brandished a paring knife. She rewarded him with a cheeky grin. "You're my hero!"

She headed out the back door.

She could count on the people in the kitchen to lie completely or to at least slow Quinn down, and she would send Brandon a text message. He'd be unhappy, but if she apologised and offered to buy him a drink the next time she saw him, he'd take good care of her instruments.

She hadn't been kidding when she'd told Quinn that Brandon was among her admirers. If he had his way, they'd be intimate. Sidestepping his concern and his advances was a constant challenge and one of the reasons she didn't always tour with the band.

Outside in the chilled evening air, she caught her bearings. The Rocky Mountains were always to the west, she'd been told. Using the snowcapped peaks as a guide, she turned right. She figured she was about four blocks from the Sixteenth Street Mall and she needed to take another right here.

She glanced over her shoulder before rubbing her arms against the cold and hurrying towards the pedestrian mall's free shuttle bus.

She kept a wary eye on the people walking along the street, and she got off the bus a stop early and took a detour to her hotel.

Fifteen minutes after she'd rushed out of the pub, the hotel's doorman greeted her by name.

The elevator was waiting, and thankfully she had no problems with the electronic cardkey in her door.

Now, her entire body collapsed against the door, pulse pounding, she exhaled deeply. That was as big a celebration as she was going to allow herself. Sinead O'Malley wasn't exactly the great escape artist.

After she caught her breath, she pushed away from the door. A hasty departure and dash through downtown was easier when you weren't at this altitude.

Sinead was smart enough to realise she'd only earned a reprieve.

She had chosen, as usual, not to stay with the rest of the band. She always chose this small, personal, funky boutique hotel rather than one of Denver's bigger hotels.

Even though she made unconventional choices when she could, staying ahead of Jack Quinn wasn't going to be an easy matter. He'd chased her for nearly two weeks with his insane idea that they should marry. When she'd read his first, formal letter, she'd scoffed. Marriage? Not now, not ever, and definitely not to a Quinn.

Still and all, she was learning he wasn't a man likely to give up easily.

Eventually she'd be back in Ireland and he would, too. No matter how clever she was, she couldn't hide forever.

Her pulse still faster than normal, she crossed to the small octagonal-shaped table near the door and dropped her handbag on top. The oversized bag had enough cargo capacity for her to make a quick escape if needed.

She dug in the cavernous depths of her bag for her mobile phone. After she located it, she checked the time back home. It was very early morning in Ireland, which meant she might wake up people.

She scrolled through her address book and dialled her mother's number. She had a calling card so ringing wouldn't cost a small fortune, but truthfully, at this point, peace of mind was worth almost any cost.

After ten rings, she punched the 'off' button. Then she rang her cousin in Murrisk, a small town in the shadow of Ireland's holy mountain, Croagh Patrick. She got a perky, annoying voice mail. Her aunt in Westport didn't answer, either. So she left another message.

Sinead told herself not to worry. Her mother might be getting on in age, but she walked every day, and was as hale and hearty as a north wind. Her aunts were in fine health, and her few cousins were young and vigorous, even if none of them had yet to produce a child. Quinn had been right. As it stood, there weren't many of her line left.

She knew rationally that if there were bad news, someone from home would ring her. She was learning, though, that when it came to worry, rational thought didn't matter. It was always possible her family might decide not to bother her while she was so far away.

If she didn't get a return call by the time she'd finished her bath, she'd start dialling again.

That settled, she sent text messages to Brandon and the rest of the band members to let them know she was safe. After dropping the mobile on the table, she pulled her shirt over her head then unzipped her kilt and wiggled out of it. In her usual manner, she left both articles of clothing in an untidy heap on the bright purple carpeting.

She was glad she'd been booked into this hotel. Its unique designs suited her. The chairs and settee were oddly shaped. The lamps and table decorations were crafted from bold geometric designs. The walls were painted primary colours, and their contrast worked surprisingly well with the carpet.

It was a good thing the pub was footing the bill. She was on tour to earn much-needed funds for her family. Her bankbook would never stretch far enough to cover this sort of expense.

Once she'd toed off her shoes and taken off her socks, she padded into the bathroom, enjoying the sensation of cool ceramic beneath her feet.

One had to love any place that actually had a bidet, she thought. Orgasm in a bowl.

It'd been so long since she'd had a climax, she'd almost forgotten what it felt like. Almost, but not quite. And after a day like today, a rush of endorphins was exactly what she needed.

For now, ignoring the bidet in favour of a hot, relaxing bath, she cranked open the bathtub's faucet and adjusted the temperature from warm to scalding. As the tub filled, she stripped off her bra and knickers.

Then, standing in the bathroom naked, she reconsidered the bidet.

How long *had* it been? Her schedule left her tired. When she wasn't on tour with the band, she ran her family's bed-and-breakfast. Turning their home into overnight accommodations and adding self-catering cottages had been the only way to save their ancestral estate. Every penny she made on the road, she sent home. So far, her family was managing, but the personal cost to her was great. She was as tired as she was lonely. But honestly, the unrelenting demands left her without much of a craving for sex.

Even if that hadn't been the case, she'd taken enough verbal lashings from her former fiancé to last a lifetime and make her wary of letting another man so close.

Donal had been everything she thought she wanted in a man. He was rich, successful, dedicated to the land and a shared heritage. He made it clear they'd live at her ancestral home, raise their children on the grounds. She wouldn't have to worry about anything ever again, and neither would her mother or other family members.

Her family had loved him; she'd loved him. They'd seen him as more than a knight in shining armour — they'd seen him as lord and saviour rolled into one.

She'd tried. Heaven knew she'd tried.

But sex had been totally, completely, mind-numbingly boring.

One night before bed he'd come out of the bathroom. He'd looked sexy, fresh from the shower, dark blond hair damp, a few drops of water still glistening on his body. He'd asked what she was reading and she'd shyly showed him the BDSM novel. The cover had a woman's bare buttocks on it, and it was clear she was turned over a man's knee.

Donal had gasped in outrage.

"Don't be filling your head with that nonsense."

She'd been embarrassed by his reaction, but she'd persevered. "Don't you ever get a bit bored by the sex we have?"

"Certainly not. And it should be good enough for you, as well."

It wasn't and it never would've been. She'd learned to fantasise and pleasure herself while he was already asleep.

A few months later, he'd got on one knee and presented her with an engagement ring and asked her to marry him immediately. Her heart had pounded wildly with dread when the oversized diamond had winked in the light.

She couldn't accept.

Despite her family's plight, despite his warning that she'd never find another man to tolerate her ridiculous ideas, she'd closed the box and returned it.

She couldn't live with his bucolic expectations. In bed, out of bed, he didn't allow her to be who she really was. Seeing the ring made her realise she couldn't pretend any longer. She didn't want to.

She had naughty urges and wouldn't settle for a life of missionary 'are you done yet' sex. She'd rather go without than endure like a martyr.

He had been clear that he wanted marriage and children and he'd wanted her to be a good little wife and raise them while he provided for his family's needs.

He'd told her to forget dancing, drumming, piping, wild, screaming, blow-your-head-off sex. On the other hand, he'd be pleased and life would be grand if she could spend a wee bit longer perfecting her Yorkshire pudding recipe.

Since then, there'd been an occasional one-night stand. The one man she'd explored BDSM with had been the only one who came close to giving her the kind of climax she wanted.

She'd told Quinn the truth of it earlier. She rarely had sex. She'd learned that one-night stands were emotionally draining. She hated the morning-after awkwardness. Over the past few years, she'd dated a few men, but rarely for longer than a couple of weeks. Her travel schedule and familial obligations made relationships even more complicated. She'd taken to wearing cheeky T-shirts as armour. Still, some men initially thought the printed sayings were a joke.

They weren't. For the right man they were an invitation.

If he could see past the wording, see what she really wanted…

She wanted a man who was persistent enough to crack her reserve, see the flaws beneath and not let it matter while she experienced the crazy carnival of lust.

Dreamer.

That's what her mother, as practical as Sinead herself, would have said.

Sinead had responsibilities and obligations, a family business to preserve. She had to be focussed, she reminded herself. Practical. None of that ridiculous man nonsense for her.

The bathtub finally full, she turned off the tap and sank into the depths. She rested her head on the tub's rim, letting the water cover her up to her neck.

And from where she was lying in the tub, she had a perfect view of the bidet.

With a sigh, she closed her eyes to block out the sight.

And she saw images of *him*, the obnoxious, overbearing, handsome Quinn.

Damn it; damn him.

She hated him, and yet she was mortifyingly aroused.

After a second sigh, she opened her eyes again.

What could it hurt?

If she had an orgasm, maybe she could stop thinking about him, stop thinking about sex, stop thinking about being across his knee while he flipped up her skirt and yanked down her knickers.

Yielding to the tempo of need drumming inside her, she climbed from the bath and turned on the bidet's tap. She dried off with a towel as the water warmed.

She checked the temperature, knowing she liked it warm. She made an adjustment then rechecked the heat before dropping the towel.

She moved into position over the water's hot stream. It felt good, but she spread her labia so she could get more pressure on her clit. She rocked her hips slowly, trying to find the pace that would take her over the top.

The water on her pussy felt sublime.

But she couldn't quite get there…

In her mind, she heard his voice, steel wrapped in velvet, as he threatened to give her a good hiding.

Those words shouldn't have excited her or thrilled her, but they had.

His eyes had darkened and there'd been a determined set to his jaw. Despite her bravado, she had no doubt he was man enough for her.

And if that hadn't turned her inside out, the smile when he'd worked his way onto the stage would have. He was clearly a man accustomed to women giving him anything he wanted.

She was determined not to be one of them.

But with his dark good looks and cool determination— crikey, he'd been a step behind her for six thousand miles without giving up—Jack wasn't like any other man she'd ever met. It was the kind of resolve that turned her on even as it annoyed the hell out of her.

The image of his eyes, lightning-intense and striking, made her weak. With a soft sigh, she held her labia apart with one hand, fingered the small nub of her clit and tilted her hips forward a little more. The warm water caressed her like a man would. *Like he would?*

And truthfully was that what she wanted?

Or did she want something more?

When she masturbated, she had fantasies of being tied up, of being helpless as an orgasm was wrung from her.

She told herself that it didn't matter if Jack Quinn were the man to give her what she craved. She'd never betray her family or herself by sleeping with the enemy, so she'd never know.

Sinead tried to chase thoughts of him from her mind. She kept her labia spread, then moved her other hand to cup her left breast and tease the nipple. The steaming water made her clit swell more and more.

She heard his words repeat in her mind as he told her that when he went home, she'd be by his side.

Ha.

Sinead made her own decisions. *Imigh sa diabhal!* The devil take him.

Determinedly, she summoned one of her favourite fantasies. She'd place her hands on her hips and face down a larger, taller man who refused to be intimidated by her. Why not? It was *her* fantasy and that meant the man of her creation wouldn't care that her T-shirt told him to bugger off. He'd be unimpressed when she told him to take a walk in short, jerky motions.

In her imaginings, she'd be abducted by this stranger and be made to surrender to his darkest desires, desires that matched her own. Sinead knew she was a strong, powerful woman, but the imagery was compelling and seductive. She yearned to have control yanked away, and yank it he would. And because she was helpless in his grasp, she could abdicate responsibility. Nothing but her pleasure would matter.

This man would claim her. Toss her over his shoulder. He'd keep her captive with his artfully tied knots and cleverly devised bonds. He'd torment and tease. He'd see through her sarcasm to her vulnerabilities. He'd cherish her, but tolerate no nonsense. He'd be the strength to the softness he'd bring out in her.

His tongue would caress her clit; he'd suck on it, lick it. He'd keep her pinned beneath him till she screamed her surrender, until she admitted he was not only her equal but her master…

He'd demand her active participation. He'd hold her chin captive, much as Jack had at the pub. Her imaginary man would bluntly inform her he would not settle for anything less than her total commitment, emotionally and physically. He would not tolerate her simply saying the words and going through the motions.

She'd blossom, become aware of her sexuality.

And—

And—

Her fantasy began to unravel as Jack Quinn once again took centre stage. She no longer saw a nameless stranger, but a frightening enemy. Quinn had stormed into her life with his ridiculous ideas, commanding presence and unsettling words.

Didn't that beat all?

She tried to shut out his image by pretending she'd never set eyes on him.

With her jaw clenched, she fought desperately for a climax, squeezing her clitoris, pinching her nipples, gyrating her hips.

And there was...nothing. Nothing at all. It was as if the building sensations simply vanished.

But then she imagined the feel of Jack's strong palm on her arse.

She gave up the fight and allowed the new images to unfurl.

Jack would hold her firmly, one hand pressed on the small of her back. He'd stroke her buttocks, and she'd become damp with need. Then, only then, would he deliver a sharp stinging slap to her rear.

She'd beg and plead, she'd wriggle, she'd protest, but he'd be relentless.

He'd torment her until she orgasmed.

Like... *Now.*

She shouted out as she climaxed. Her entire body trembled with the overwhelming power.

Her hips continued to jerk as aftershocks assailed her.

Finally she drank in several gulps of the mile-high oxygen-depleted air, trying to restore her breathing to normal.

Bastard.

Damn the man and sentence him to half a dozen centuries in purgatory, anyway. Couldn't she even masturbate in peace? She for sure wouldn't be lighting a single candle to save his unholy soul.

Her lips curled around a very nasty curse and she yanked the faucet closed. If she ever got her hands on him…

He *was* Satan incarnate, just like his pesky ancestors.

The water droplets that had fallen from her hair chilled on her shoulders and she climbed back into the bathtub and sank in up to her chin, desperate to wash away thoughts of him.

With her eyes closed, she heard a sound.

A soft wailing came from next door. So much for her rest and relaxation.

After pulling the plug to drain the tub, she got out and slipped into a big, fluffy robe the hotel had thoughtfully provided. A few sips of whisky from the minibar might help take off the edge so she could sleep.

In the living room, Sinead stubbed her toe.

Could the day get any worse?

She knelt to grab the object, probably one of her own shoes, carelessly strewn about.

Her heart stopped. Then her pulse slammed into her throat.

A comb.

Sinead wiped a trembling hand across her mouth as she stared.

She couldn't make herself bend to pick it up. Just like the one he had, this was silver, probably sterling, with an ornate inscription that resembled her family crest.

The Banshee myth had many variations. In some she was an old woman, in some, a young one. She combed her hair in some. A silver comb was a herald of death, and so was a weeping, keening or wailing…

34

Dear God.

The wailing from next door!

Sinead shivered. She wasn't superstitious, but damn...

The Banshee only followed certain families. Including hers.

Standing, she backed away from the comb.

Breaths short, she dashed across the room for her mobile phone. She scrolled to the call log and pressed redial on her mother's number. When there was no answer, again, Sinead redialled. "Pick up," she ordered. "Pick up, pick up, pick up." The phone rang without answer. She swore, ended the call and determinedly pressed redial.

Finally, finally, her mother picked up, sounding tired, groggy, and a wee bit annoyed.

"Sinead?"

"I found a silver comb, Ma."

She knew her ma would remember that all combs had been banned from their lives. This was serious.

"I was sleeping like the dead, if that counts," her mother said.

She scowled. "That's not funny, Ma."

"I was sleeping," Bridget repeated. "Until you woke me up."

Realising how ridiculous it all seemed, she apologised.

"We're all fine here, dear."

She remembered all the times in her childhood when her mother had told her to pull her head out of the clouds and stop dreaming.

"Enjoy your time in America. Have fun on your tour. It does you a world of good to get away."

"But—"

"Stop your worrying, love. Now unless you're going to have a handsome young man brew me a cup of tea, I'm going back to bed."

Sinead was quiet, not sure what to say next.

"Anything else, Sinead?"

She hadn't told her mother about Jack Quinn chasing her halfway around the world. She'd kept the entire situation private from her family, not seeing the sense in worrying them. Now she wished she'd have said something.

Explaining that his grandmother had found a comb and that the man himself was insisting on marriage would be a lot for her family to accept.

"Sleep well, Ma." After a final apology, Sinead rang off. She'd thought that talking to her mother would help, but she was still unsettled.

Ignoring the comb, she continued to the minifridge and pulled out a small bottle of alcohol, priced about four times more expensive than it would have been in the shops. Desperate times called for desperate measures.

She decided right then that she would install these tiny well-stocked fridges in her family's cottages. They were a heck of a way to make money.

She twisted off the cap and drank straight from the bottle. Tonight, more than any time in her life, she was in need of the fortification from a belt of good—or even bad—Irish distillate.

Unsure of what to do, she rested her hips against the windowsill and stared at the silver comb. It seemed to wink menacingly in the overhead lights.

She couldn't go back into the bathroom to brush her teeth without stepping over the damn thing.

She hated to admit it, even to herself, but she didn't want to touch it.

And how was she supposed to sleep knowing it was there?

Calling housekeeping to come and remove it seemed absurd, but maybe...

She was barely surprised when there was a knock on her door.

If it had been anyone from the hotel, housekeeping or the front desk with a message, they would have announced themselves.

For about thirty seconds she debated what to do.

She was on the fifth floor, so going out of a window wasn't an option. She could call hotel security and have him removed, but she knew he'd wait her out.

And damn it, the fact she'd found a comb upset her and he was likely the only person in the United States who would understand her agitation.

After that sensual fantasy, part of her wanted him, every bit as much as she wanted not to want him. Her shoulders slumped.

He knocked again, a determined, forceful sound. "I know you're in there, Sinead. Open the goddamn door."

She didn't ask how he'd found her. He hadn't travelled six thousand miles and traipsed across two continents to turn around and go back home when she ducked out the backdoor of a lower downtown Denver pub.

She should just be glad it had taken him this long.

Temporarily beaten, she exhaled a shaky breath and placed the small bottle of liquor on the windowsill. She pulled the belt tighter around her waist and checked to be sure no cleavage showed.

She should stall him while she dressed, but she doubted even a suit of armour would offer protection against the man.

She opened the door, and he took her breath away.

Damn but she wished she didn't have to hate him.

His arms were folded across his chest. He wore a brown leather bomber jacket and he leaned against the jamb as if the room were his own. Just like the man of her fantasies, he had that rakishly long, dark hair and his was a bit tousled from the wind.

Despite her best intentions, Jack Quinn's devastating good looks and piercing blue eyes weakened Sinead's knees. Oh, aye, not everyone would find him handsome, she supposed.

Beaten by the wind and weather, he was as rugged as a gale off the north Atlantic. His nose looked as if it had been broken in a rugby match. And it would be rugby. This one wasn't as lean as footballers. He was broad as a ship's bow, hewn by the elements.

His eyes, though, unnerved her.

Deep, dark blue, the colour of the sky as the moon rose. He stared at her unblinkingly, as if seeing into her soul. Despite how warm she was from her bath, she shivered.

"I told you we weren't finished yet."

Chapter Three

She sighed. At times she might be reckless, but she was never stupid, and she knew when she was beaten. And truthfully, despite the fact she didn't believe in fairies and fae and getting luck from kissing a rock, the discovery of the damn fecking comb bothered her.

"Invite me in."

She took a reluctant step back. Then she squared her shoulders. He might be here, but this was her room, and she was in control. "You'll make a racket otherwise, I suppose."

"Your hospitality is charming." He crossed the threshold then hung the Do Not Disturb sign on the handle. He closed the door behind him and slid the safety bolt into place, locking them in the room together.

In the small area near the door, he dominated the space. With his broad shoulders emphasised by the leather jacket he seemed so much more overpowering than he had at the pub.

"Truth be known, you gave in far more easily than I thought you would. I wasn't sure if I was going to have to bribe the manager or sleep in the lobby."

"I—" Her voice cracked and she cleared her throat before trying again. "It has nothing to do with you."

"Surprise, that."

"I, er…over there." She pointed. "Silver comb." She hadn't meant to tell him that. She'd meant to be cool, competent, dismissive, maybe even abrasive.

She waited, braced, for his sarcasm. She'd deserve it, too. She was overreacting to something that likely had a logical explanation. Although he said nothing, his brows knitted together in concern.

Why the hell did he have to be so nice? "It might not mean anything." Who was she trying to convince? The one he found might not mean anything, but this one surely did. "The cleaning people could have dropped it. That might not be my family's crest on the back." She hadn't looked at it close enough to be sure.

Then she heard it again. A soft, keening cry.

His brows rose. She shuddered.

"You've telephoned your family?"

"Everyone's safe." She exhaled. "My ma says I should enjoy my time in America and finish the tour with the band. Honestly we need the money. Ma's not superstitious at all. In fact, generally, neither am I. There's honestly no need for me to go home, but…"

"You're concerned." His voice was soft, sympathetic. In contrast, he was large with shoulders broad enough for both their worries.

If she were a lesser woman, she might be tempted to lean on him. And he was broad enough, strong enough, to carry her burdens. "I've been on the road constantly over the last few months."

"I know. I had a hard time keeping up with you."

She wasn't sorry to have put him through a lot of effort. If he'd left her alone, he could have been at home relaxing. "I'm probably tired and overwrought."

"Is that how you are, Sinead?"

She exhaled. When she answered, she was truthful. "No."

"Maybe there's something to all this bad blood between our families. And you and I have a chance to do something about it."

She should have known he'd take the opportunity to try to convince her to do what he wanted. "Thanks. No. I have enough responsibilities to the future without worrying about the past."

"I've got an aeroplane waiting."

His own damn plane? While her family scrimped and saved? "Don't keep it waiting," she said. "Feel free to put your miserable soul back on it and jump back across the pond. I'm certain the world is waiting for you to resume control."

"Stop fighting it." He lowered his voice a few octaves, and the deep richness of the sound made a sensual thrill slide straight to her female bits.

"Stop fighting me." His voice was an odd combination of encouraging and demanding. "You're coming with me, Sinead. By fair means or foul."

She was suddenly glad he'd shown up. She'd gone from frightened to furious in less than two minutes. She feathered back her damp hair and glared. "Listen, Mr—"

"No, Ms O'Malley, it's you who will listen." He took a step towards her. "Two continents, six thousand miles, dozens of telephone calls and e-mails. You, woman, will be going home, with me."

"Bugger off."

"Sharp-tongued wench, I meant it when I said I was done listening to you. You're coming home with me. Will you do it willingly, or no?" He unfolded his arms and took another step towards her.

She backed up instinctively. But she had enough wits about her not to move towards the bed that so thoroughly dominated the room.

"And when I get you to Eire, if not before, I'm going to fuck you senseless."

He moved so quickly then that she didn't have time to react.

He took her by the upper arms and moved her back three full steps. "And I'll make you call my name as you come, screaming."

He let go of her but shock immobilised her. When she found her voice, she looked up at him and laughed, with more confidence than she truly felt. "I'll call you many names, *diabhal*. But it won't be from anything intimate, I promise. The likes of you isn't getting anywhere near me."

Jack's nostrils flared. "The likes of me?"

"Descendent of murdering bastards," she clarified recklessly. "The Quinns weren't good enough for the O'Malleys eight centuries ago. You're nowhere near good enough now."

The cold fury in his eyes shocked her. She recognised she'd overstepped the bounds of his good nature, but she stood her ground, even when he took a large stride in her direction. She kept her head tilted back, unsure whether she was being brave or just stupid.

On one hand, if she made him angry enough, he might decide she and the O'Malleys weren't worth the effort and he'd leave them the hell alone. On the other, antagonising a lion was rarely a good idea.

Viciously he encircled her upper arms once again. He dragged her onto her toes and against the solidness of his masculine body.

His lips found hers, demandingly, punishingly.

The latent passion, eight hundred years of anger, flared in an instant.

A slow throb uncurled between her legs, just like the one during her earlier fantasies.

He forced her mouth apart, and their tongues met.

He was warm, insistent.

She worked her hands between them and pushed against his leather-covered chest. The man was unmovable.

He thrust his tongue deep into her mouth. She parried, as if they were sparring.

But he was relentless.

With his kiss, he dominated her.

Her body betrayed her with a rush of desire.

There was something between them, 'twas as if they'd met before. She knew him. And he knew what she wanted.

No other man had ever been so uncompromising with her.

Her breaths became ragged as she fought her need to surrender. Abruptly, he ended the kiss and released her. There were no gentle nips. There was no softness, nothing to show that he desired her.

Her emotions went arse end over tea kettle. She suddenly, ridiculously, felt rejected. She wanted *more*.

What was wrong with her? They were enemies, had been for centuries. "I'll thank you to keep your hands off me in future.'

"With that body of yours? No fecking chance."

She folded her arms across her chest. As if that could protect her from him.

"I've had a taste, Sinead, and I want more."

Even though there'd been no soft words, he wanted her in a carnal way that made her senses whirl.

"And you want me."

"It's cold in here. Hell must have just frozen over."

He raised a brow.

"If you're thinking I want you, hell froze over," she added, just in case he'd obtusely missed her meaning.

"Your mouth is far better used for kissing than talking," he said. "Much sweeter that way."

He moved fast.

He had her arms uncrossed and pinned at the small of her back before she could blink. He imprisoned both of her wrists in one of his callused hands. She fought, but she couldn't get away. In fact, he brought her closer to his body.

His strength was nearly overwhelming. His chest was solid. And his cock was hard, pushing demandingly against his jeans and against her belly.

She shouldn't want his possession, but she did.

The small struggle had made the robe's lapels part slightly. Her breasts were thrust towards him, and her nipples had hardened. Most upsettingly, her pussy had moistened with arousal.

"Not much to say now, hey?"

"Release me."

He relentlessly held her gaze. He wasn't stupid; he knew she was having a physical reaction to his touch.

He traced a finger into the V where the robe's material overlapped.

Her breaths became even sharper.

"Tell me you don't want my touch."

"I don't." Even she barely recognised the sound of her own voice.

"Tell me that convincingly."

"I..." Oh, aye, she wanted his touch. More than anything, she wanted to *not* want it.

Still holding her prisoner, he tugged on the knot of her belt.

"Unhand me, you unholy bastard."

The belt fell apart, the ends dangling at her sides.

He wouldn't...

"Your skin is so soft, Sinead. Inviting."

"The invitation isn't for you, Quinn."

"Oh aye; yes it is. I'm the only one here," he whispered, his hoarse voice throwing her into a seduced trance. "Here with you. I can hear your breaths. I can smell that heat that comes off you. Pungent."

"You're crass."

"The smell is all woman, Sinead. Like you're in heat."

She was going to drown in a sea of her own mortification.

"I'll bet, when I part this robe, that your breasts will be full and your nipples hard. Any bets, Sinead?"

"*Fuck you.*"

"Yes.That's exactly the idea. I'll fuck you. Then you can get on top and fuck me."

She wanted to tell him not to touch her, but her damnable body betrayed her. When he moved the robe

45

back across her shoulders, her breasts were heavy, and her nipples were pebbled.

"You have beautiful breasts," he said. "And your nipples…"

He cupped her left breast and gently squeezed.

"How much pressure do you like on your nipples?" he asked.

"Don't…"

"A little? Or are you as tough as you want people to believe you are? Is it only an act, Sinead?"

This time she didn't answer; she couldn't find her tongue in order to speak. It had been so long since a man had touched her, she was hungry for anything, the gentlest of touches or something wild that ignited her.

While he held her breast in his palm, he brushed a thumb across her nipple. It tightened a little more.

"Maybe a bit more pressure?"

She closed her eyes.

He gave a gentle squeeze that he instantly released.

"Oh God," she whispered.

"Too much?"

She shook her head, even though she felt as if she were betraying herself to the enemy. She hadn't known she liked this kind of intensity. Even the one man she'd been with who was more adventurous than the others hadn't stimulated her nipples this much.

Quinn did it even harder.

She sucked in a breath, but she didn't object. She'd never had a man apply that much pressure before, and damn, she liked it, the pain with the pleasure.

He eased up a bit and she tried to move towards him. His hands and the way the robe had fallen back off her shoulders restricted her movements in a way that aroused her even more.

"Ah," he said. "Have you ever worn nipple clamps?"

Through her haze she asked, "Nipple clamps?"

"You'll become intimately acquainted with them."

Then he squeezed her tortured little nipple hard and for a long time.

Moisture pooled between her legs. If he'd known she was aroused earlier from her scent, there'd be no doubt now.

She whimpered when he released her.

Then, dizzyingly, he grabbed the nipple again, viciously pinched it and pulled it up and away from her body.

"Definitely clamps," he said.

He released her nipple then moved so quickly he shocked her. He shoved a hand between her legs to cup her feminine mound. He tightened his grip against her cunt. She screamed out an instant orgasm. Still holding her wrists, he eased her towards him.

Her legs were weak, and she offered no resistance.

"I had no idea you were so perfectly responsive."

She drew a few shaky breaths before realising her cheek rested against his chest, against the leather jacket warmed from his body. He still held her pussy, and his thumb was possessively on her thigh.

She was all but naked while he was fully dressed and demanding sexual responses to her.

"Don't fight." He released her wrists and wrapping his right arm around her, holding her intimately still, as if she were a lover.

She stiffened.

Suddenly, no matter how much she'd wanted it, how much she'd willingly surrendered, she was angry...with herself, with him.

She pushed away his hand and ducked out from under his arm. She moved towards the window, away from him as she frantically struggled back into her robe, trying to reclaim her composure as well as her dignity.

The distance helped the haze of delirium to fade and she thought about what she'd done...what *they'd* done. "You took advantage of me." She furiously knotted the belt and yanking the lapels over each other.

She expected his outrage or upset or denial. Instead, he laughed. The arrogant bastard had the nerve to laugh.

"I took advantage of you?" he asked. "Are you implying that this is not your cum on my fingers or that you didn't shamelessly grind your cunt against my hand?"

"Don't be so crass."

"That wasn't crass."

He started across the room towards her. She involuntarily stepped back before freezing in place, refusing to be intimidated.

He advanced on her. Despite her resolve, she retreated. He backed her up against the wall. He had her trapped. There was a purposeful gleam of intent in his eyes.

"This," he said, "is crass..."

He trailed his still-damp fingers across her lips. She'd never tasted herself before, and while it wasn't totally unpleasant it was outside of her experience. The man unnerved her.

"We both know that you want me to finger-fuck you, right here, right now. But saying it aloud would be crass."

Damn, did he have to look so good, smell so good? And did the rough sound of his voice have to turn her on?

"Didn't your beloved *máthair Chríona* teach you any manners?"

"None... None whatsoever," he added cheerily. "Which means I have no qualms about kidnapping you."

"Doesn't much matter what the country is, kidnapping is pretty much illegal."

"Pack your bag. You're returning to Eire with me."

"You really don't care at all about niceties."

"Not at all," he agreed.

"If you think I'm going anywhere with you after...after that, you've lost your senses. If you ever had any to begin with. Unlike you, I have responsibilities to my family. I intend to finish my tour first."

"Your part of the tour is over."

Infuriated by his arrogance, she reacted by shoving her forefinger into the centre of his chest. Not that that was such a good idea. She felt his strength. He was solid. All muscle and tendons and sinew...and man. This close, she inhaled the scent of sea and land and determination — close to a millennium of determination. "You see here, Mr High and Mighty, Lord of All He Surveys, I am going nowhere with you." In her anger, she continued, "I know it's completely impossible for you to understand, but my family needs the money I make on tour. Aye, I love playing with the band, but I do it mostly because I have to. I need to."

"Sinead, I'm not the monster you'd have me be. As my wife you'll go short of nothing."

"This isn't about me, you thick-skulled Neanderthal. This is about my family, my mother, my cousins and their children."

"I'll see them short of nothing, either. Now pack your bag," he repeated. "Else you'll leave here in your robe" —

he reached for the tie, fingered the end—"or, better, completely naked."

"Have you not heard a word I said?" Tipping her head back, she looked at him through narrowly slit eyes. "You really are an arrogant bastard."

"Right, then." He picked her up and slung her over his shoulder. Within a few steps, they'd reached the door. He slid the safety lock open. Then he opened the door to step into the hallway.

Her cheeks heated. Anyone could see her. "Stop!" Blood rushed to her head, making her dizzy. The world, the entire fecking world, had gone mad. His shoulder, softened somewhat by the buttery leather, dug into her. She grabbed hold of his belt loops to maintain her balance.

The soft, sad keening came again. She shivered. She was well aware of the comb, ominously dominating the middle of the carpet. "Please."

"You'll get dressed then?"

She wanted to be back in Ireland. In spite of her mother's reassurances, she wanted to be home. Truthfully she'd well and truly decided to abandon the tour. And this way, she wouldn't have to pay the airfare. "Put me down this instant."

Time stood still. And so did the blasted Irishman.

"I'm waiting for an answer."

She thought she was stubborn. But this man could out-stubborn a mule. "Yes. I'll get dressed and pack my bag. Now put me down."

"You might want to be trying on some manners, Missy."

Or beat the hell out of his back, for all the good that would do her.

"Put me down. Please."

Before he did, he flipped up the hem of robe and delivered a sharp slap across her bottom.

She yelped with far more effect than the smack warranted and she tried to tell herself he hadn't just fulfilled a fantasy. "You're a complete arse, Quinn."

"Manners, Ms O'Malley, manners. Be lucky you didn't get more. You earned it."

Through gritted teeth she said, "Please put me down."

He did, and not gently at all. Breath whooshed from her and her knees wobbled.

Sinead made a mad dash for the bathroom, taking care to avoid the blasted comb.

"Earlier, at the pub," he called out, "you were generous enough to give me two minutes. Now I'm returning the favour."

She slammed the door behind her. Before she could turn the lock or smile triumphantly, he shoved the door open, nearly knocking her off her feet.

"Happy to help, if'n you need it."

"Piss off."

"Leave the door open."

"I need a little privacy."

He allowed his gaze to sweep down her body. "I've already seen your lovely self."

"I need a few minutes' privacy," she repeated. "I have some personal things to attend to."

"Do it with me standing here or not at all. You'll not be getting any privacy. You haven't earned it."

"Earned it? How dare you?"

He grinned, a man with the upper hand.

"You'll be getting no quarter from me, wife-to-be. You've given me the shrift through half a dozen American cities, and it was fecking hot in Chicago. I got drenched in rainstorm in Portland. I nearly got mowed down by a taxi in New York. You dashed out the back of a pub, and another of your bloody fans in the kitchen tried to hold me back with a knife."

She blinked. "He did?"

"And that wide-eyed pup Brandon gave me a false hotel for you. If you think you're shutting another door on me, think again."

The man might be infuriating, but he wasn't stupid.

"Two minutes, Sinead."

Saying nothing else, he looked at his watch.

She sighed in utter frustration. She'd spent her adult life dreaming about being with a man who was her match, a man who wouldn't put up with any nonsense, a man who was big and strong and capable. Now that one stood here, his foot positioned so she couldn't slam the door a second time, she was finding the reality wasn't nearly as appealing.

She gathered her toiletries from the marble countertop and dumped them into an oversized cosmetic bag. If he seriously had his own aeroplane, she probably didn't need to worry about making sure the liquids were kept in a separate plastic bag. And if they were flying commercial, he could bloody well wait while she dealt with security. "If you'll excuse me." She swept past him.

She grabbed her suitcase from the floor and tossed it on the bed. She'd flown in earlier from Kansas City, and she'd played a couple of sets. She was tired, and she didn't want to deal with this overbearing male. "Can't we leave in the morning? This is ridiculous, starting a transatlantic flight so late at night."

"If that's what you want," he said. "I'll make the arrangements."

She narrowed her eyes suspiciously as she looked at him.

"I am trying to be reasonable.,"

"What's the catch?"

"No catch," he said. "The bed is perfectly big enough for both of us." He shrugged out of his bomber jacket and dropped it on the edge of the mattress. "And the room is paid for."

"Never mind," she said. In his tight black T-shirt, he was even more dangerous. And when he pulled the hem of that T-shirt up, she all but salivated. But, Christ, did he have a nice, tight-looking abdominal area.

"Never mind?"

"We can fly tonight," she said.

"Or we can fuck in this big bed. Not saying you'd get much sleep."

She grabbed a pair of jeans and a long-sleeved shirt from her case.

He picked up her discarded clothes from the floor where she'd left them scattered.

She tried not to be embarrassed by him handling her bra and knickers. After all, he'd had his hand between her legs, and he'd brought her to a shattering orgasm. She grabbed her tartan and T-shirt from him, but he held onto her underwear. Could this day get any worse? "I can pack my own clothes," she said.

"I'd wondered," he said quietly.

She looked at him.

"If you had on a bra beneath that T-shirt while you were onstage. I could see your nipples from halfway across the pub. Do you know how many men were lusting after you?"

Their eyes met.

"Aye, lass. Including me. I couldn't wait to get my hands and my mouth on you."

While he put her laundry in the zippered part of her case, she pulled out a pair of black knickers and a clean bra. This whole situation was bizarre, surreal. Her enemy was packing her bag while she was pulling out fresh clothes. They stood close enough that their arms brushed and she inhaled that clean, crisp scent that was uniquely him.

She thought of trying to wriggle into her knickers while she was still wearing the robe. Then she decided against it.

She placed all the clothes she was going to wear on the bedspread.

She tried not to notice that her hands shook as she fumbled with the belt. It took three tries to unknot the blasted thing.

He collected her dance shoes from the floor and stuffed them into her case then yanked the zip closed before folding his arms across that broad chest and shamelessly watching her.

She shrugged and allowed the thick terry cloth to fall to the carpet.

"Lovely. You've the body of an athlete."

Under his appreciative gaze, her nipples had once again hardened. Her pussy was still damp. No matter how they fought or how much she intellectually hated him, her body responded to his masculinity.

She grabbed the bra from the bedspread.

His eyes darkened and he reached out, taking her by the shoulders.

"You're mine," he said.

"Never."

He cupped both her breasts. Then he stroked both nipples with his thumbs. The nipple he'd squeezed earlier felt tender, but in a way that made her instantly respond.

"Damn, but you've a responsive body."

Her knees buckled. Instinctively she grabbed for his wrists to hold herself steady.

She hated this push and pull of emotions. She wanted him, and she desperately wanted not to want him.

He stunned her then by kneeling in front of her. *No*.

She kept her legs together.

"Don't deny me."

"I will." Again and again. No matter what her traitorous body wanted.

He released her breasts and she released her grip on his wrists.

Then determinedly he worked his left hand between her thighs. "Your pussy is drenched."

"A natural enough reaction."

"So that's the way it's to be?" He slid a fingertip across her clit. Then he pushed, hard enough to wring a gasp from her. "Means nothing to you, Sinead?"

"Sex is sex. You can get it on any street corner."

"And this?" He began to rub.

She forced herself to stand still instead of swaying with the motion. Damn there was something appealing about having such a large, forceful man on his knees, his mouth a whisper away from her cunt.

Abruptly, he slid a finger inside her.

Christ. He shocked her, but he didn't hurt her. It felt...

He inserted a second finger inside her.

He looked at her, then pulled them out and showed her his fingers, glistening with her juices. "Means nothing," he repeated.

"Are you trying to prove a point? Trying to prove that the Big Bad Evil Quinn is a lady's man? Is that what this was about? *Fillean meal ar an meallaire.*" Evil returns to the evil doer.

He stood and caught both her hands, imprisoned them behind her back and forced her body against his, her tight little nipples abrading against the cotton of his T-shirt. "That wasn't evil. This..." He captured her mouth in a quick, brutally tender kiss. "This isn't evil, either."

She looked up at him, aware of her nakedness and his full state of dress, his aura of command.

He knelt and easily slid both fingers back inside her.

She moved then, her body betraying her mind. She spread her legs to accommodate him.

"Shall I do you like this till you scream?"

He gave her no time for an answer.

"I think that's what you'll do. Scream. You're not one for a quiet climax are you?"

Not gently, he parted her labia then moved forward and captured her clit between his teeth.

Oh God, how long since a man had eaten her pussy?

Deliberately this man was undoing her resistance, with his combination of pain that brought her to the brink of tormented pleasure.

He licked her, he nipped at her. She started to whimper. Then he pressed his tongue against her. She jerked her hips. She moaned. Her soft little sounds grew louder as he finger- fucked her in addition to licking and sucking.

She curled her hands into the thick locks of his hair, dragging his head closer. She was so close, almost there...*almost.* "I want to come," she admitted.

"And I want you to beg for it," he said, words muffled by her heated flesh.

He pulled back and removed one finger from her pussy. She felt him move the moist finger backwards so that he was probing against the entrance to her arse. She'd never done this before, but…*yes*…

"Tell me.Tell me you want my finger in that tight little hole. Beg me to finger-fuck both holes."

"Quinn. I can't."

He continued to torment her just a little, not enough to get her off.

She jerked her hips in response to his finger, his mouth, his tongue. Oh God, his tongue…

Then he stopped."Beg."

Her body felt like a tightly-strung instrument. "Yes," she said. "Yes. Please."

"Beg," he repeated.

"Please finger-fuck me, Quinn."

She'd never used such graphic language before. But with him, it didn't embarrass her. "Please…"

"The words, Sinead. I want to hear the words."

"Please finger-fuck me."

"Not just my cunt, but my arse."

Hot colour chased up her cheeks. "Finger-fuck my cunt, my arse."

"And your clit, Sinead? What do you want me to do with your clit?"

"Lick it, suck it."

"Tell me it all."

"I want…" She cleared her throat. She was a performer. She'd been on stage since the age of five. She knew how to step out of reality and into an alternate place. This was really no different, despite the fact it was her enemy kneeling in front of her, his masterful mouth only a breath away from her most intimate place. "Please, Quinn. Finger-fuck my cunt and my arse while you lick my clit."

"Do not come without permission," he told her.

"I beg your pardon?"

"That's how things will be, Sinead. We'll be using clamps. I'll tie you up. In the bedroom, hellcat, you'll be mine. If you're very good, I'll let you climax. But never, and make no mistake about this, without permission. If you come without my approval, it'll be a long, long time before you're allowed another one."

She was barely able to think. In spite of his sensual but harsh words, he hadn't stopped touching her. And Lord help her, she didn't want to make him stop. An orgasm churned deep inside, and she wanted the release it would bring.

Earlier, on the bidet, she'd had a tiny release, nothing compared to what he'd given her a while ago while he tormented her nipples. But even that, she knew, would be tame compared to what was building now. Every muscle and sinew felt stretched tight, demanding satisfaction. "I'm not sure what kind of women you've dealt with before," she told him, "but I'm not one of the simpering villagers where you rule like lord and master. You can't tie me up or force me to beg for your sexual favours."

"Oh, aye, lass, I can. And you'll do it of your own free will. You'll crawl to me with bindings in your teeth and you'll drop them at my feet and beg me to secure you to a punishment bench."

"Punishment bench?" Was he serious? He couldn't make this up, could he? "You sound positively medieval."

"Quite the contrary. My punishment bench is modern. The hooks are brand new."

"I'll see you in hell first." But because the picture he painted was so close to her own fantasies, she shivered.

"Love, you'll be happy to make the trip."

Brutally he slapped her cunt.

She gasped. She was horrified, not just because of his vicious act, but because she was so incredibly wet.

"Do you like that?" he asked.

"Not on your life."

"Your mouth tells one story," he said. "Your body tells another. You were made for me, Sinead, for my mastery. For my lash. Come without permission and you'll feel the wrath of my belt across your arse cheeks."

Oh God. Had it been less than an hour since she'd imagined herself across a man's lap, his hand falling repeatedly on her naked buttocks? Had he used magic to read her mind? Or did he truly mean it?

She told herself she needed to end this immediately, get out of here, maybe call the police. But her feet felt as if they were encased in concrete. Instead of turning away, she rose onto her tiptoes, wordlessly seeking more. She had no idea what was happening to her, why she was responding so completely.

He nipped at her clit and she squealed. "No coming without permission," he reminded her. "Do you understand?"

She was still reeling from the smart smack to her swollen vulva. Her entire being throbbed with need. It would take him thirty seconds, maybe less, to make her shatter. "I'd rather crawl through molten rocks."

He laughed, and the vibration only stimulated her. "My rules. My way. Yield now or I'll leave you on the edge."

Bastard that he was, she knew he'd do just that. If she were a stronger person, she'd shove him away, put on her clothes, and figure out another way to escape. But with him on his knees, his mouth right there, she was not only willing, she was weak. Damn him, she didn't want him to stop.

"Shall I continue, Sinead? Shall I give you the orgasm of your life?"

Her breasts were full, her nipples had swollen. Her breathing was laboured.

"It's your choice entirely."

"Make me come," she ordered.

"What happens if you come without permission?"

"A spanking." She rolled her eyes even as she wondered what that would feel like.

"One you won't forget," he said. "Take your hands out of my hair and place them behind you. Cross your wrists at the small of your back. Pretend they're secured, and don't move them. We'll consider that you're tied by my will."

"You've lost your senses."

"Five seconds to comply, wench."

She shuddered. She knew he meant it, and damn it, the rush of heat between her legs told her that her mind was rebellious, but her wanton body wasn't.

Slowly she disentangled her hands from his hair and obediently did as she'd been told.

"Stick out your chest just a little more to arch your back. That'll give me greater access to your hot little cunt."

Feeling humiliated, she did exactly what he ordered.

"I forgot what you wanted."

Liar.

"Tell me again, in detail."

"Please, Quinn," she said, "I want to come." As she spoke, he started to move, rewarding each word with a tender stroke. "I want you to finger-fuck my cunt..."

He moved a finger slowly inside her, as he might thrust his cock. That was enough, she knew, to bring her off, given enough time.

"And my arse," she whispered, desperate to wrap her hands around his head for support.

"Anal virgin?" he asked.

"Yes," she confessed. "A bit nervous."

"We'll go slow. And when we're home, I'll give you some time to adjust to wearing a plug."

She might have protested if she could have found her voice. But she knew there'd be plenty of time for arguing later.

She felt his finger begin to press into her anus.

"Tell me what else," he said.

"Lick my pussy. Lick it good."

"How much pressure against your clit?"

She couldn't believe they were having this conversation. It was simultaneously erotic and mortifying. "A lot. "I sometimes can't..."

"When you masturbate?"

"Yes. I have trouble..." He pressed his tongue against her — hard — as he shoved his finger inside her rectum.

Sensations assaulted her, feeling as if they came from the inside out. She was delirious with desire. One of the most gorgeous men she'd ever seen, was licking and sucking her cunt, fingering both holes while she panted.

She rocked back and forth, thrusting her pelvis forward, shamelessly demanding he give her more. He responded perfectly, as if intuitively reading her body's needs.

The sensations built and built to a primal crescendo.

She was on the balls of her feet. She wanted to reach for him, but she recalled his words, that she was tied by his will. For reasons beyond her, she wanted to please him as much as he was pleasing her. He wanted her hands behind her back. She'd keep them there. "Quinn!" She remembered, barely. "Please," she said. "Please. I want to come. I need to come."

He didn't respond. Instead, he continued to eat her, lick her. He moved the finger inside her arse.

She was helpless, undone. "I'm begging. Begging. Let me come, Quinn."

He murmured something that she prayed was assent.

Screaming like the Banshee herself, she came, hard.

She was unable to keep her balance, despite the fact he moved his shoulders forward to support her thighs. Her toes sought purchase in the carpeting, but it wasn't enough. Defying his order, she grabbed his shoulders and pulled him forward, grinding her cunt shamelessly against his face.

He continued to lick, to suck, to fuck until the last shudder passed.

Her knees felt weak, and she couldn't draw a breath all the way into her lungs.

As if in slow motion, he moved, gathering her into his arms, sweeping her from the ground and carrying her to the bed. He placed her there, on the side opposite the suitcase.

Now that the ordeal was over, she felt vulnerable in her nakedness. She reached for the robe, but couldn't quite curl her listless fingers around it.

He left her, and she heard water running

He returned less than a minute later with a warm, damp flannel that he placed between her legs.

She had never had a man tend her like this, and she liked it.

All fight had left her, even though she knew he was a Quinn. Now that she'd had a world-class orgasm, the sweat on her body began to cool.

He moved the piece of luggage onto a nearby chair then toed off his boots and sat on the edge of the bed.

She eyed him warily.

"You didn't follow my orders," he told her.

She stiffened, aware of her state of undress and the fact his jaw was set in an uncompromising line. Butterflies roiled in her stomach. "I asked for permission when I came," she whispered.

"You didn't keep your hands behind your back."

"I was going to lose my balance, you bastard."

"You were given an order. You'll be punished for your transgression." He reached across the bed and smoothed her hair, brushing strands back from her cheekbones.

What the hell was wrong with him? He was soothing her, even as he threatened her.

She reached for her robe and dragged it over her. She sat up and scooted away, pressing her back against the headboard.

She saw that his cock had hardened. His threat turned him on. Sick sod.

So what did that say about her that her pussy moistened slightly at the idea of him punishing her? She tried to rid her mind of the thought and all-too carnal images. But part of her wanted to know what he had planned. Part of her hoped he wasn't just tormenting her.

"Get your sweet little arse across my knee."

In a very American way, something she learned from Brandon, she said, "Bite me."

"Right, then."

He moved fast. Before she knew what he was about, he'd stood and grabbed her. The robe fell onto the carpet. Despite her flailing, he effortlessly managed her. As if she weighed nothing, he sat back on the edge of the bed and turned her over his knee.

She learned her lesson about goading him.

His denim jeans were scratchy beneath her bare skin, and she was aware of the power and strength of his thighs. He was all man. Strong. Unyielding.

She desperately fought for balance, and before she found it his hand came down—hard—on her arse. "Curse you a hundred thousand times!" She kicked her legs futilely.

He placed a hand firmly on the small of her back and spanked her again. This one wasn't as hard, and in fact it wasn't totally unpleasant.

She tried to ignore the little voice that reminded her that boring sex and conventional expectations were some of the reasons she'd ended the relationship with Donal.

She'd wanted to experience more.

He stroked her pussy. "You're damp." He slapped her right butt cheek again. "Cease your struggles and we'll end this after two more."

She nodded weakly. She could do this. She wanted it.

"Put your hands behind your back."

"How will I balance?" she demanded, the words muffled because of her position.

"I'll make sure you don't fall."

"I'm to blindly trust you, am I?"

"You're being punished because you didn't keep your hands behind your back," he reminded her. "Next time perhaps you won't forget."

She knew right then that he was giving her a choice. She might call him names, he might truly be an ogre — with a wart on his nose and all — but he'd made certain she was aroused.

He was as good as his word. He moved a big hand to the side of her ribs and gave her support while she brought back her arms.

"Clasp your hands just above your buttocks," he instructed.

She shifted her weight so that she was more balanced on the balls of her feet.

Once she was positioned, he moved his hand to the centre of her back. "How many more?" he asked.

"Two. You said two."

"If you cease your struggles," he reminded her. "Otherwise we can keep going. It's up to you, *a rún*."

She could do anything for that short a period of time. Caution to the wind, she challenged, "Bring it on."

He laughed. "Reckless little thing, aren't you?"

Before she had the chance to answer, he brought his hand down across both buttocks. She yelped and her right foot came off the ground. "That fecking *hurt!*"

"I imagine it did. It stung my hand."

She bit back another reply, realising it wouldn't get her far.

"Settle yourself and let me know when you're ready for the next one."

"It'll be the last one," she corrected. Her thoughts were becoming fuzzy with all the blood that had rushed to her head.

"If you take it well," he agreed blandly.

"It's the last one," she bit out.

"Let me know when you're ready."

"Do your worst."

She braced herself, tensing her buttocks, but the final blow was nearly gentle. He'd placed it directly on top of the previous one and the sensations ignited her response. She was on the verge of another orgasm.

Instead of pleasuring her like she'd hoped, he helped her to her feet.

She swayed for a few seconds, but he kept a steadying hand on her. The man was pure genius when it came to arousing her. And at the moment he was a pure torment when it came to satisfying her.

"How was your first spanking?"

She might have snarled if she had the energy. But truthfully the man had fulfilled a naughty fantasy. It had been everything she'd imagined. No wonder she'd had trouble finding a man to settle with. She'd been restless with plain man-on-top until he got it done—a couple of minutes if she were lucky—sex. This, this had been so different. He'd been all about her pleasure. Crikey, he hadn't even undressed. But no way would Sinead admit the truth to Quinn. He'd grin or gloat, maybe even both. Then she'd have to kill him.

"I'll be looking forward to your next beating."

"You're the only one," she lied.

Tenderly he smoothed back errant strands of her hair. "You're so much more than I expected."

His opinion of her didn't matter...or at least that's what she told herself.

"I see why a man would be willing to risk his life to fall in love with an O'Malley. Come to bed, Sinead."

He snagged her wrist and drew her towards him. She thought he might kiss her. She was disappointed when he didn't. "You can sleep on the settee."

"That's one lesson well learned now, lass. I always sleep in the bed. Fuss and fight all you want, but I'll never give up a bed. I'd prefer you sleep in the bed with me, but I'll ring for an extra blanket it you're preferring the sofa."

She was short, but the settee didn't look all that comfortable to her, either.

"I'll thank you to stay on the far side of the bed."

"I'm sure you would." He grabbed her robe from the floor and tossed it over the back of a nearby chair.

"I'd like to sleep in that."

"You'll sleep nude to dissuade you from dashing out the door."

Did he think of everything?

He left on his own clothes and climbed onto the bed. He lay next to her. "Rest. You can fight me later," he said. "And I'm certain you will."

Without allowing her the luxury of arguing, he held her. He had one arm around her waist; he pressed the other just above her pubic bone. In this position, her buttocks were nestled against the firmness of his pelvis.

The flight might be over for now, but the fight would begin anew as soon as she had the energy. She'd not allow the Quinn *diabhal* to have power over her body or her mind. Nor would she be his bride.

But a naughty, naughty part of her wondered if he was as good with his dick as he was with his fingers.

Telling herself she'd never find out, that thoughts like that were dangerous and led nowhere, she tried to wriggle away from him, even by just a few centimetres, but he was relentless in this just like everything else. Without saying anything, he simply held her even tighter.

Chapter Four

For the first time, Jack thought that perhaps *máthair Chríona* knew exactly what she was doing by inviting an O'Malley into their ancestral home. Well, not exactly inviting, he mentally amended. It wasn't as if Catherine had suggested they have Sinead to tea. *Máthair Chríona* was all but asking Sinead to be the home's mistress.

Catherine was convinced that they had the chance to end the bitter feud once and for all. By marrying Sinead and having babies with her, eight hundred years of angst could be laid to rest.

Until now, he hadn't been convinced.

He didn't believe in curses and Banshees any more than Sinead did. He would have never taken time out of his business and followed her but for one thing: seeing his *máthair Chríona* happy.

When Catherine had found a comb with the O'Malley family crest on it, she'd seen it as a sign. Why else would something from the O'Malley clan appear in her very own bedroom?

After nearly a millennium of fighting, of kidnappings, of stealing, of sabotage, Catherine was convinced it was her obligation to put an end to the curse. If she had to manipulate and cajole her grandchild, so be it. She had the chance to leave a legacy, and by hell, she was going to do it.

When he'd protested that there was no such thing as a curse, she'd put her hands on her arthritic hips and glared at him as if he were once again a naughty child in short pants. "Perhaps not, my boy. But are you gonna deny that there's bad blood between the O'Malleys and the Quinns?"

He'd shaken his head.

"Or that our family started it?"

Again, he'd shaken his head.

"Then it's fitting that we should end it." She'd dropped her voice then. "Then that's that. You and I, my boy. We're the only ones who can. That makes it our obligation."

His entire life, obligation had been drilled into him. It was the reason he'd got an education, the reason he always returned to the lands. The Quinn legacy was in his hands, and he'd heard that from the time he'd been in the cradle.

"So what's the harm in marrying the lass? You're over thirty, now. It's high time you help shape the future."

Máthair Chríona was right about a number of things. He was in his thirties, and it was high time he married.

This was no longer the middle ages and he wasn't required to produce an heir. Even if he had no children, the home would go to a cousin...but the nearest relation wasn't a man he particularly liked. And if he stepped outside tradition and left the estate to another cousin, the legal battles would keep the home's future tied up in court.

Máthair Chríona, until now, had been tolerant enough to leave him to his own devices, especially the last few years since Maeve. Since Maeve's betrayal, he'd enjoyed his bachelorhood. He'd dated plenty of beautiful women. And he'd engaged in consensual BDSM with many.

Despite *máthair Chríona's* patience and hope, he'd found no one else he wanted to marry. His grandmother had recently been insisting that Maeve had broken his heart. He didn't believe in broken hearts any more than he believed in leprechauns. The fact was, none of the women he'd been with in the past few years had held his attention long enough to even consider asking his grandmother to open the family vault so he could select a ring for a bride-to-be.

Still and all, burying an axe, making *máthair Chríona* happy and settling down all in one move was smart and strategic. There was only one flaw in the plan. Sinead herself.

The petite and athletic woman was filled from the tips of her toes to the top of her lovely head with vim and vinegar.

She clawed and scratched, but she had a submissive side, of that he was sure. Putting up with her shenanigans would make the times she purred all the more spectacular.

Jack grinned as he felt her slowly, slowly, relax against him.

The wench fought her own responses as much as she fought him. The dossier hadn't prepared him for the reality.

His *máthair Chríona's* men had even interviewed people familiar with Sinead, but even that didn't tell the whole story.

She was passionate and wild. A hellcat. But when his mouth was on her hot little mound, she purred like a kitten.

Behind his jeans, his cock throbbed. He wanted his dick in her, wanted to fill her pussy and pound into her.

Then he wanted to fill her arse, stretching that tight hole for his penetration.

No matter what passed her appealingly sweet lips, Sinead liked things the way he did, over the edge, as untamed as the land they both called home.

Honestly it hadn't been his idea to marry her. And even if he'd been forced to write up a list of eligible and appealing women, her name wouldn't have been on the list. Still, if he had to be burdened with one, especially an O'Malley, it might as well be her. There were many advantages financially, despite the fact her family was struggling. The O'Malley lands adjoined his and he had the resources to turn around her family's fortunes.

He didn't fool himself, though. She'd be a challenge from beginning to end.

He looked forward to taming her.

And if she kept up with the mouthiness, he'd gag her.

Shite. That idea nearly made him ejaculate without even touching his cock.

The zip of his jeans chafed. Teach him to leave off his boxers now, wouldn't it?

He felt more than saw the gentle rise and fall of her chest as she drifted off to sleep.

He lifted an imaginary pint. She wouldn't admit it, but this round had gone to him.

As soon as he was convinced she was completely asleep, he got out of bed and picked up the silver comb. Indeed, it was her family's crest on the back. He placed it inside his jacket pocket, along with the one his *máthair Chríona* had found.

He exchanged text messages with his pilot, making sure the woman was prepped for an early-morning departure. After that, still feeling restless, probably from the denial of an orgasm his body craved, he climbed back into bed.

It took all his resolve, and turning down the room's temperature several degrees, to keep his clothes on. Through the years, and by many people, he'd been called arrogant. The truth was, he was. But he decided he wanted to see her on her knees, sucking his cock, making it hard and wet, before he claimed her.

That decision hadn't stopped his shaft from standing to attention the entire damn night, however.

Although dawn approached, she still slept soundly, and he let her. He'd kept her covered, kept her warm, kept her close.

He wasn't a fool.

He knew he'd pushed her sexual boundaries last night.

His grandmother's people had interviewed several of her former boyfriends. One idiot had called her frigid. And indeed, the barkeep had said her nickname was the Titanic.

The man she'd nearly been engaged to, Donal, had come closest to uncovering the truth. When he'd been interviewed, he'd politely mentioned she had some unusual tastes that he'd done his best to put a stop to. He'd stopped short of using the word 'perversion'. But obviously his tight-arsed opinions had something of an impact on her.

Since then, she'd obviously kept her passion on a tight leash. Maybe it scared her. Or maybe she'd never been with anyone man enough to bring it out in her.

Because of her interest in BDSM, he could see her being bored by most men, by most of her sexual experiences. But Jack Quinn wasn't most men and he had tastes she'd never even dreamt of. She might consider herself kinky, but she had no idea.

Most of all, she didn't scare him, despite her quick tongue. In fact, he found that one of her more endearing qualities.

She might not realise it, but he'd been there for her last night after her first ever spanking. He wasn't sure how she would react She could have felt panic, guilt, or maybe she'd have a unique reaction. He wouldn't have been surprised if she had been angry.

She'd slept hard, though.

At one point, right before the heater had kicked on, she'd shivered. He'd tucked the blankets around her shoulders.

In sleep, her defences had been down. She'd snuggled against him. Her hand had curled into the material of his shirt. She'd never do that if she were awake.

He murmured soothing words, encouraging her to rest.

Within seconds, she'd settled again.

The lovely Sinead was going to be the perfect submissive. She distrusted him now, but she'd learn, eventually, to rely on him.

Finally knowing they risked running late for their flight, he reached over and switched on a lamp.

"You're a beast. "Turn off that light."

"We've a plane to catch."

"Are you still about that nonsense?"

In answer, he moved quickly. In moments, he had her naked body pinned beneath his. "Oh, aye, I'm still about that nonsense." He grabbed her arms and pinned her wrists above her head. "Or I can keep you here all day and fuck you until you can't stand."

"I thought you were going to be a gentleman."

"A gentleman? Compared to what's driving me right now, I am being a gentleman. And you should be grateful."

Her mouth opened just a little. He was more than tempted to kiss her deeply. She looked so very lovely with her eyes still hooded from sleep, her hair mussed around her face. It'd been a long time since he'd woken in bed beside a woman. And the idea of waking next to her appealed on so many levels. "Now you've got two choices. You can get dressed and I can get you a cup of tea—"

"Stuff it. I don't drink tea."

"What are you, uncivilised?"

"Too uncivilised for the likes of you. So you can feel free to turn your back anytime, and I'll just slip out the door. Might save yourself from harm."

Nay. Now he'd found her, he wouldn't be letting her go. "Then I'll just have to see about some coffee," he offered.

"Cream and sugar." She licked her upper lip. "And a pastry."

"You drive a hard bargain."

"Chocolate something."

He rolled his eyes. "I was rather hoping you'd select the second option that I never had the chance to make." He moved against her suggestively. Despite her protests, she'd spread her legs a bit. Even through his jeans, he felt the heat that radiated from her body.

"I'll stick with the coffee and the pastry. Option number two probably has something to do with your body being naked, seeing as how you've woken up with a hard-on, and really, I have no desire to have any part of you inside me."

Her comment might have deflated his ego, but it had absolutely no effect on his morning erection. In fact, her challenging words served to raise his libido a couple of notches. "I think you liked your spanking. I think you secretly want another."

"I think I want coffee and a pastry, a chocolate pastry, else I'm going back to sleep. You can be a bully at a more civilised time. Like noon." She yawned.

"Not a morning person, then?"

"For you, not a morning, mid-morning, noon, afternoon, evening, and especially not a night person. Now get off me, you big lug, and get my coffee."

"Lucky I'm not bleeding from all the wounds your words inflict." Round three to the lass from Westport.

"You have no idea how lucky." She glared at him.

No wonder she frightened the men who wanted to bed her.

He rolled off her, but before leaving her, he flipped her over.

She squealed, all girl. "What the hell are you about?"

"Seeing how red your arse is from last night's spanking."

She reached back to cover her buttocks, but he imprisoned both her wrists.

"You could have taken quite a bit more." Her skin was barely pink in a couple of places. "I'll give you another hiding later, one that'll last longer." Just having her in this position made his cock massively, ragingly hard.

Before he forgot himself and kept the plane waiting all day, he nipped her right buttock then released her, delighting in her gasp.

He grabbed the phone and punched the button for the front desk. He requested a toothbrush for himself, coffee for both of them, a pastry for her, and he added they'd be leaving in about half an hour and would need a taxi.

Keeping her body angled away from him, as if that could lessen his ardour, she wrapped herself in her robe.

"Leave that bathroom door open a crack," he called out when she slipped from the bed and headed across the room, "else I'll take it off the hinges. And yes, I would."

Her response was earthy, and a four-letter word, no matter the language.

Still, she was a smart woman and she was learning. She left the door open a crack.

While she freshened up, a bit difficult he imagined as she'd already gathered up her toiletries, he grabbed toothpaste and a hairbrush from her bag, before organising her clothing so the bag would actually zip shut. Seemed the woman was a disaster at taking care of her stuff.

Moments later housekeeping arrived with his toothbrush. She promised the coffee would arrive shortly, and they'd deliver it in to-go cups.

Her eyes widened at the sight of the tip he gave her. 'Twas worth every penny if it made Sinead happy.

Sinead might think him an ogre, but he waited for her to finish up. It wasn't until after he heard the toilet flush that he pushed opened the door.

He stopped short and stared, entranced. His woman was taking a bidet.

Her back to him, she was crouched over the water's spray, her labia spread, her hips angled forward. If he didn't miss his guess, she was halfway to an orgasm, one he hadn't given her permission to take. They'd certainly be discussing that later. For now, he just wanted to see her get off.

"What the hell do you think you're doing barging in here?" she demanded, looking over her shoulder. Her voice cracked and her face turned red, from her jaw to her cheeks.

"We need to be accustomed to sharing personal space, and I need to freshen up before we go to the airport." He continued into the room, rubbing the shadow on his jaw. "I could do with a shave, but it can wait until we're on the plane. Carry on with what you're doing."

"I..." She dropped her right hand to the knob to shut off the water then reached for a towel. "Christ on a stick, Quinn."

He squirted toothpaste on the toothbrush, as if catching her on the brink of an orgasm was an everyday occurrence. In the mirror, he looked at her.

"I was just cleaning up."

"Don't let me stop you." He made a mental note to have a bidet installed in every bathroom he owned.

"I—"

"I'll tolerate no shyness between us," he said. He splashed water on his hair and face. His kingdom for a razor. "Your choice, Sinead. You started down this path. Turn that water back on and continue to masturbate, or I'll turn it on for you. And if I do, I'll make sure you're not only clean, but that you have multiple orgasms."

Her eyes widened. "You'd..." She stumbled for words. "You'd..."

"In fact, that's a marvellous idea." He dried his hands on a towel.

"Oh, no you don't, you scoundrel."

"Your choice, *a rún*."

My dear? He was calling her *my dear*? He had nerve. She gritted her teeth. "Fine. I'll do it myself."

"More's the pity."

He dropped the towel and regarded her.

Her eyes were wide and her cheeks were still red. She appeared both embarrassed and aroused by his earthy demand.

As he waited with infinite patience, she turned the water back on and adjusted the temperature before closing her eyes and rocking her hips. She held her labia apart with one hand, and she slid the index finger of her right hand across her clit.

The water's spray and her positioning made it impossible for him to see as clearly as he wanted. But watching her reaction was enough for him.

As the orgasm built, her head tipped back, and her fiery blonde hair spilled over her shoulders and down her back.

She moved her finger faster and faster and her hips all but gyrated.

He couldn't help himself.

He moved in closer and stood behind her. He reached around her to cup her breasts. As her breaths became desperate gulps for air, he flicked his thumbs across her nipples, making the nubs even harder.

"Jack!"

"Aye." Damn but his cock was hard as a mountain. He hoped that when he finally fucked her he'd last longer than a teenager.

"I'm there," she said.

She was asking permission, he realised. *Shite*. He could ejaculate without even touching his dick at this point. "Come for me, Sinead."

Her vulva was reddened from the heat, and she jerked against the spray. He couldn't be more delighted with her. His worst nightmare wasn't a woman like Sinead. His worst nightmare was a woman who was cold, unresponsive, even frightened. But this defiant she-devil? He looked forward to the challenge of conquering her.

She screamed out.

Like he knew, she wasn't one for polite little orgasms. They were drawn from deep inside her. And they turned him on.

She seemed to lose her balance, and he was there, releasing her breasts and holding her around the waist to steady her.

Instead of shoving him away, she grabbed on, her fingers digging into his forearms. She dragged breaths through her partially opened mouth rather than her nose.

If he had his way, he'd keep her fulfilled all the time. She was a sexy, sexy woman.

She blinked, as if returning to herself. "That was..." She trailed off. Then she tried again, "hot."

"*A rún*, you've no idea how hot you are." Or how fecking much he wanted her. Holding her with only one hand, he reached for a towel. "Allow me."

He turned off the bidet then he patted her between the legs, drying the water.

There was a knock on the door, followed by a cheery, "Room service!"

"That'll be your coffee."

"And a pastry?"

"I value my life."

She took the towel from him. "I'll just finish up in here."

He paid the woman and gave her a generous tip. Not only were the coffees in go-cups, but an assortment of pastries had been placed in a paper bag.

"Your taxi should be here momentarily, sir."

Sinead came out of the bathroom, and as the other woman closed the door behind her, Sinead dropped the robe and reached for the knickers he'd laid out.

It was as if, momentarily, they had a normal relationship, not one of snarling and gnashing of teeth.

She shimmied into her thong, and the only thing he was thinking was how to get her back out of it.

She fastened her bra in place then pulled on her jeans and another T-shirt while he shamelessly watched. This one had a graphic of a hair dryer and a saucy message to accompany it: This blows.

He might have thought she'd bought it intentionally.

"Is that coffee for me, or are you holding it hostage?"

"Cream," he said. "And sugar." He splashed a huge dollop of cream in the cup and stirred in several packets of sugar.

"If that one's mine, it needs to be sweeter."

"Jaysus, woman. Your teeth'll rot."

"Good. Maybe it'll keep you from trying to kiss me."

"No chance. You'll have your mouth full of my dick every chance I get." He carried her coffee to her. "You can join me in the bathroom while I brush my teeth."

"You've lost your senses."

"I'm taking no chances with you, Sinead. I don't trust you for a moment."

"If I promise not to dash out the door?"

"Into the bathroom with you."

She scowled, but she accepted the coffee. She didn't say thanks—she just wordlessly preceded him into the small room. "I'll tell you right now, if you decide you want to use the bidet, I'm so out of here, even if I have to jump out the window."

"Oh, my cock needs a good wash, but it'll be your mouth doing it."

She choked on her coffee. He gave her a good pat on the back that nearly lifted her off her feet. While she fought for breath, he brushed his teeth.

"I'll not make you stay in here while I use the facilities. But this much is clear, Sinead. If you're not sitting on the bed when I come out, I will tie you to the bloody seat on the aircraft." He levelled a gaze at her. "Clear?"

"You're a bastard enough to do it."

"Believe it."

When he returned to her, she was sitting on the edge of the bed eating a pastry. He wasn't sure whether or not he liked her behaving. "Did you save me one?"

She grinned and popped the last bite into her mouth. "No."

"You ate them all?"

She licked her fingers. "They were delicious. I hope you're not too hungry."

His stomach gave an on-cue groan of protest.

"And if you don't hurry, I'll have your coffee, as well."

The phone rang. "That'll be the taxi."

She stood and shoved her feet into a pair of sandals.

"Over my shoulder?" he asked. "Or will you walk like a good girl?"

"Good girl? *Good girl*?" Her mouth opened like a fish out of water.

He'd caught her off guard, maybe even pissed her off a bit. He extended the handle on her bag and started towards the door, grabbing his coffee from the table on the way.

He opened the door for her. "You need to know, Sinead, it's always your choice. I'll treat you with the respect and trust you earn. But I do rather enjoy you being over my shoulder with my hand on your arse. You might spill your coffee, though."

She tossed her hair like royalty and breezed past him to punch the elevator call button. She moved all the way to the back of the car, as far away from him as possible. In a move that was sexy as hell but something she hadn't done intentionally, she propped her gorgeously shaped buttocks against the brass rail.

The illusion that they'd been a couple had been just that—an illusion.

* * * *

Jack was a master of understatement.

He didn't own a plane; he owned a jet. The plane was more than transportation, it was home and office and pub rolled into a luxurious package.

She sank into a ridiculously soft oversized seat. It was more like an armchair than a standard airline seat. It didn't hurt her backside, still a bit tender from his late night spanking—despite the fact he said her derriere wasn't red. It might not look abused to him, but it felt a bit that way to her.

She wasn't really sure what she thought of the spanking. Being over his knee, his powerful hand falling on her exposed arse, had been more of a turn-on than she'd imagined, and she'd had high expectations from her first spanking. Still, she was annoyed. Why did he, of all people, have to be the man who finally gave her what she wanted?

"The seat reclines." Jack stowed her baggage in a small closet that had plenty of shelving. "A footrest will pop up as you go backwards. Much better for circulation."

She noticed there were no overhead bins on this plane, presumably so that someone as tall as Jack could stand comfortably.

"Something to drink, Ms O'Malley?"

She looked up as a middle-aged man approached them. He was a very good-looking gentleman, with a shock of silver hair and a quick smile. He wore an apron over his button-down shirt and navy-coloured slacks. "I'm Aonghus, and I'll be taking care of you during the flight."

Another surprise. She expected Jack to employ young, sexy females. But a man...? She wished Jack weren't so complex, wished she could pigeonhole him and dismiss him as being shallow. "Coffee?" she asked hopefully.

"Use half a container of creamer," Jack said as he shut the closet door. "And a full bag of sugar."

She scowled at him.

"A bit of coffee with your cream?" the man asked.

She smiled at the attendant.

Jack took a seat next to her. "I'd pay good money to see a smile like that directed at me."

"You'll be waiting a while."

She'd never travelled like this. In all her travel with the band, she'd never even had an upgrade to first class. She was accustomed to the least expensive seat on a plane, and it seemed she was most often miserably shoved into a centre seat, especially on transatlantic flights.

Because she could, she stretched out her legs.

"A pastry, ma'am?" the attendant asked, returning with her steaming cup of coffee. "We'll have breakfast available as soon as we're airborne, but in case you need something to hold you over…?"

"We have croissants, I believe," Jack said, raising a questioning brow in the man's direction.

"Chocolate and plain," the attendant confirmed.

Chocolate? She wouldn't be dancing much in the upcoming days until she was back in Ireland and could get away from Jack by fair means or foul, and she'd already had several pastries. Really, she shouldn't. But what the hell? She needed energy to deal with Quinn, and if breakfast had protein, it would cancel out the effects of the carbohydrate overload. Or that's what she told herself. "You've talked me into it."

"Chocolate," Jack told the man.

The attendant smiled at her.

"And I'll have a bloody Mary."

She could easily get accustomed to this, she realised. Being treated like a princess suited her.

Too bad there was no prince in the picture, only a very rich toad.

Despite the fact she'd already had more than enough sugar, she accepted the porcelain plate with a pastry the size of a small country. Some people travelled with real silverware and china?

She picked up the croissant and bit into it. Almost-liquid chocolate oozed into her mouth. Oh *yes.* Not only was the pastry gorgeous, rich, buttery and flaky, but it had been warmed. She could definitely get used to being treated like this.

The captain came out of the cockpit to greet them.

She wiped her fingers on a serviette while Jack stood to greet the woman.

Wasn't the man a study in interesting contrasts? A black woman piloted the craft, a hunky man waited on them. From what she knew of Jack, he was fairly traditional, but the first people she met stood that stereotype on its head. That he wanted to spank her and fuck her wasn't a shock, but his other choices were.

Sinead put the plate on a table and shook the pilot's hand.

"It's a pleasure to meet you, Ms O'Malley," the pilot said. "You've led us on quite a merry chase across the States." While still retaining her professionalism, the woman smiled at her, as if in solidarity. "I've seen airports I didn't know existed."

"She's a wily one," Jack agreed.

"I look forward to being of service to you in the future."

Sinead narrowed her eyes at Jack. Just what the hell had he told his people about her?

"I hope you and Mr Quinn have an enjoyable flight. Do let us know what we can do to make you comfortable."

As if being treated like royalty wasn't enough?

Once the flight attendant notified them it was safe to be up and about, Jack excused himself.

She flipped through a magazine and looked out the window. She'd been kidnapped. Well and truly.

Every part of her chafed at the indignity. Her entire life she'd made her own decisions, and her family, God bless them, had encouraged her independence. Now to have a man dictating to her… *Shite.*

He returned a few minutes later. She looked up with a scowl.

"Such a beautiful face, with such an unpleasant expression."

Standing in front of her, he reached out and captured her hair in one unyielding fist. He held her tight, but not unpleasantly so.

"Let's see what we can do to see your mouth partially open, your lips swollen from my kiss."

"No…"

"There are far better uses for your mouth than to deny me."

His hand still in her hair, he moved towards her.

Damn.

He stopped just centimetres from her face.

He smelt crisp, of spice. He'd obviously freshened up, and his jaw was freshly shaven.

He'd donned a clean shirt and a khaki pair of slacks. He looked corporate and masculine and in charge. Her blood slowly heated and her mouth parted a bit. She had trouble drawing a deep breath. She cursed her own feminine reaction. She'd never had a man drag this kind of response from her before. Up until now sex had been fine, all right, even enjoyable. But this man kept her on simmer all the time.

"Open your mouth," he ordered.

"No."

"Open your mouth to me, Sinead."

He stared at her intently. She read determination in steel blue eyes and the set of his angular jaw. He tightened his grip on her hair and pulled her head back slightly. She resisted the impulse to touch his face. Her fingers seemed to itch with the need to feel his smooth skin.

He licked the exposed column of her throat.

Dampness flooded her thong.

Damn him.

Slowly he started over. He kissed his way up the side of throat.

By the time he nipped her chin, she'd willingly opened her mouth.

He thrust his tongue in her mouth. God. She was lost. He tasted of mint and man. He ran his tongue across her teeth, a gesture more intimate than any man had ever been with her.

His kiss went on endlessly, tasting, encouraging, demanding, simulating the intensity of his sex act.

By the time he ended it, she realised she'd curled her hand into his shirt, as if hanging on for dear life.

She'd arched her back, silently asking for more.

"You'll beg me for this."

Terrified he might be right, she didn't respond.

His inflight phone rang.

She blinked as he released her hair slowly, behaving like he had all the time in the world. He traced her bottom lip with his thumb. "It's swollen. As it should always be."

While he took his seat and answered the call, she knit her hands together to stop them from trembling.

He talked on the phone, powered up his notebook computer and moved a table into position to spread out a pile of papers. He ignored her. That annoyed her as much, if not more, than his constant attention and demands.

Jaysus. Was she fickle?

The flight attendant had been nowhere around while Jack accosted her, but now that they were settled, the man refreshed Jack's Bloody Mary and brought her a cola in a proper glass. Sugar and caffeine in one handy package.

Jack's fingers seemed to move nonstop over the computer keyboard. She glanced over to see that he had a web browser open. "E-mail? You're looking at e-mail?"

"Wi-Fi," he explained.

"Have you thought of everything?"

He turned in his seat and looked at her. "I'm thinking about little save having your sweet cunt."

She blushed and sucked her cola through her straw.

What was it about him that could turn her insides molten with only a few words?

"I've a conference call," he told her, reaching for the phone. "Shouldn't take more than half an hour. I'll try not to disturb you."

She nodded

She'd always seen him as the hated enemy, if not a devil, then maybe a grotesque stone gargoyle, but never as a real person with an empire to run. Truthfully it didn't endear him to her.

She and her family worked hard, and they'd had to make compromises along the way. Their lands were now shared with anyone who booked into one of the cottages, and she worked diligently to keep those places rented. She and her cousins were the handymen, the marketing department, the reservations department, gardeners and the cleaning crew when needed while Jack Quinn commanded his parts of the world from the Earth's atmosphere with fresh coffee at his disposal.

She put on a set of headphones he provided and reclined her seat slightly. Even the sound from the in-flight television and addition of the headphones weren't enough to drown out the deepness of his voice.

She flipped through all the channels and there was an obscene number of choices. When nothing intrigued her, she started over again. She had a difficult time focussing on anything except her emotions. She generally read or slept or composed music while flying. But her thoughts were turbulent, and she was having trouble clearing her mind.

Since the devastatingly handsome and determined Jack Quinn had shown up at the pub last night, her life had been turned on its axis. If he had his way, it would be a permanent state. And what in the hell was she supposed to do about it?

She debated calling home and letting them know she was on her way back from America. But what would she say? That the Quinn had kidnapped her? Wouldn't that go over well with their bad blood. And they'd certainly not endorse a marriage if they knew the truth of it.

If she said she cut her tour short because she was worried about the comb, her mother would scoff. Her cousins would be supportive. But damn it, they needed the money.

If Jack were telling the truth, that she wouldn't have any financial worries if they were married, where did that leave her?

She'd be a whore to a man whose family she hated. *Some choice.*

Amazingly fast, they landed in New York. The flight attendant told them there would be a layover, hopefully of less than two hours while they refuelled and refreshed the cabin.

She and Jack were warmly welcomed at his private club where they were plied with more food and alcohol.

Everyone travelling was dressed posh, and she was beginning to regret her choice in T-shirt. Still, Jack didn't order her to change. Of course, if he had, she probably would have dug in her heels.

"Would you like to go for a walk?" he offered. "We can get outside for a few minutes."

She wanted to object on principle. "You could go alone."

"Not on your life." He smiled at her as if her motivations were transparent. "We'll sit here and have another round, then. Getting you slightly drunk has some pleasant implications."

She sighed. Did he always have to win? "I'd like to take a walk," she admitted.

"That wasn't all that painful now, was it?"

Her jaw ached from clenching her teeth.

He grabbed a bottle of water before guiding her outside.

New York was stinking, blazing hot. The sun scorched and the humidity drenched. The tarmac all but seemed to melt beneath their feet. "Jaysus," she said. "It's not supposed to be this hot at this time of the year, is it? Isn't it early autumn?"

"On the calendar," he agreed.

She was ready to be home, feeling the coolness of the breeze and the crisp autumn air.

They walked around the area. The private airport obviously catered to the world's elite as well as hobbyists. Planes of all types taxied and took off while a steady stream landed. At times the planes would be met by limousines, and other aircraft would disgorge passengers who headed to the terminal. One couple was met by a woman carrying a large umbrella to protect them from the sun. She'd had no idea this type of world existed.

Fifteen minutes later, they stopped in the terminal's shade. He uncapped the water bottle. She looked at it longingly.

He offered the drink to her before taking a sip himself. She chugged half the bottle before returning it to him. He didn't even wipe the rim before taking a long draught.

The act seemed somehow emotionally intimate. Lovers routinely shared food and drink. Enemies didn't.

He placed two fingers in the small of her back and guided her towards the terminal. He opened the door for her. The man had manners in public even if he were a beast behind closed doors.

While she glanced at the flat screen televisions broadcasting international news and the latest stock market results, he checked in with the pilot. Once assured the flight plans had been filed and everything was in order, he turned to her and said, "Your chariot awaits. Shall we?"

Within minutes, they were airborne.

"It'll be late when we get home. You might as well try and rest. There's a bedroom in the back where we'll have some privacy."

She turned in her seat to look at him. "A bedroom? You seriously have a bedroom?"

"Transatlantic flights are long. And flights to Asia can be just as wearing."

"So, I can go to sleep, and maybe when I wake up this nightmare will be over?" She smiled sunnily.

"Maybe I'll wake up and you'll be a pleasant companion instead of a shrew."

Direct hit. She flinched from it, even though she knew the retort was well deserved. She wondered what it would have been like if they'd met under different circumstances, if their families didn't share eight hundred years of hatred and bloodshed. What if she'd been at a bar and met a rich, gorgeous hunk who wanted to take away her problems and fuck her senseless?

He reached over and unfastened her safety belt. "I've waited long enough for you."

She'd never admit it, but she wanted it, too. "You've work to do, don't you?"

"You're my focus now. I want to woo my future bride." He stood and pulled her from her chair. "And I've decided I want you to suck my cock."

Chapter Five

She blinked and her stomach plummeted. He was raw and crude. And it made her wet. "Silver-tongued devil. No wonder you have to kidnap women."

"Baby, you'll be begging for my cock in your mouth."

She would have rolled her eyes if she weren't afraid he was right.

He snagged her wrist and led her towards the back of the aircraft.

The bedroom was smallish, with barely enough room for a double-sized mattress. But the fact was, he had a flying bedroom.

The room also contained a few built-in drawers and a small wardrobe. He could emerge from an eight-hour flight and be ready for business.

He closed and locked the door.

Alone in his domain, only centimetres separating them, inhaling the scent of his power, his gaze intent, she was no longer as brave as she had been.

"Take off your T-shirt."

"I will not."

"Remove it, Sinead, else I'll rip it from your body."

She gasped. "You wouldn't!"

"Try me, *a rún*." He reached for her.

She knew he would. No matter what threat, what promise he'd made, he followed through. "Wait!"

"You'll strip for me?"

"This is under duress."

"Is it?" he asked. "Is it really?" He traced a finger across her jawbone, then down her cheek, then down the side of her neck. He paused at the hollow.

He continued to hold her gaze captive.

He moved his finger lower, between her breasts.

Slowly, methodically, he placed his palms beneath her breasts and cupped their weight. Even though she wore a bra, she felt the heat of his touch. Through the fabric, he teased her nipples to arousal.

Her breaths became shortened as he squeezed her breasts and her nipples.

"More," she whispered.

He complied

Her knees weakened. "Yes."

He placed a thigh between her legs and leaned closer to her. She tipped her head to one side and her hair fell over her shoulder, exposing the back of her neck to him.

He kissed her gently, then sucked slightly. She knew it might leave a small mark, but she was beyond caring.

When she was almost there, he murmured, "Under duress, Sinead?"

"Say what you will, Quinn, but leave your leg where it is!"

He chuckled and the sound slid down her spine in an erotic rush. She grabbed him by the buttocks and humped his leg.

"Yes," he encouraged then continued to lick and suck and gently bite the tender part of her shoulder.

The intensity built again and he mercilessly yanked on her nipples.

She screamed out her orgasm.

He released her breasts and, like a gentleman, he held her while she regained her footing. It wasn't easy with the floor vibrating beneath her and her emotions on heightened alert.

"You came without permission."

Through an almost drugged-feeling haze, she looked up at him. "You're on about that again?"

His jaw was set. His eyes were blazing with heat. "Most certainly. Rules are rules, Sinead."

Despite the fact her body still reverberated with the after-effects of such a powerful climax, his words aroused her.

He continued to hold her about the shoulders. "Now that we've established that this isn't under duress, that you desire my body if only to hump it and get off, I'll see you naked. Five seconds to get that T-shirt off."

He slowly released his grip and took a step back, as if to better enjoy the show. Her fingers shook as she grabbed hold of the fabric and pulled it up. She might have protested that this was under duress, but suddenly, she did want to see him naked. And if his penis were as spectacular as the rest of him, she wanted that inside her.

Of course, she warned herself, she might be disappointed.

After all, he was as rich as Hades and still single.

"You've got a frown all of a sudden. What are you thinking?"

"Just wondering if your dick is as big as your ego." She decided to be honest. "Or if you're just going to disappoint me."

"Woman, you'll be the death of me."

One could hope. "You are good with your fingers. Thank God."

"You'll get spanked for your cheekiness," he warned. "Three seconds on the T-shirt, love."

She pulled it up and over her head before letting it fall onto the edge of the bed.

"Now the bra."

"Is this a strip show for your personal enjoyment?"

"It is."

A shiver chased from her toes to her shoulders.

She reached behind her and discarded the bra.

"You'll not hide your breasts from me anymore. I like looking at your tits far too much."

She knew the word was meant to shock, and it did. But it didn't offend her. With other men, immature imbeciles, she'd rolled her eyes and made comments about their maturity. But Quinn was different. He meant no schoolboy offence. It was more a masculine reaction of appreciation.

"Your nipples are still swollen."

From his touch.

"Now your jeans and thong. I'll have you completely naked."

Silently she nodded.

She kicked off her sandals. They went under the bed. She unbuttoned the waistband of her jeans and slid the zip down. The jeans, in order to fit her waist properly, were a bit snug around the hips, and she wiggled the material down her legs. She snagged the denim from the floor and tossed it across the edge of the bed with her T-shirt.

She didn't wait for him to coach her to remove the thong. She simply obeyed his wordless command. She hooked it on her finger. He nodded for her to place it with the rest of her discarded clothing.

"More's the pity it's not medieval times and I can't keep you nude in my rooms. I'm beginning to see why my ancestor thought to marry yours."

"The centuries have passed, but not your ways."

"Apparently," he agreed easily. "This spanking will be different. You'll be near the edge of the bed on all fours to start then you'll put your head and breasts on the mattress. You'll keep your knees apart so I can slap your cunt if you can't behave and stay in position."

The world seemed to go black.

"Now take my cock out of my pants."

She gaped.

She shocked herself by obeying.

She reached for his belt and unfastened it.

"One day you'll ask me to whip you with that."

She momentarily stilled. The scent of the leather, the suppleness of it, took on new meaning.

She considered a smart retort then chose to ignore him. Verbal sparring only seemed to arouse him more.

Even behind the fabric of his khaki slacks, she could feel his turgid arousal.

She lowered his zip then pulled down his pants. He'd obviously donned a pair of boxers when he'd dressed. The front was tented, gaping. And there was no doubt about the size of his cock. The man was perfectly proportionate in every way. Though she wouldn't tell him, she wanted him inside her stretching her out.

He toed off his shoes. She tried not to think of the implications, but she squatted so she could pull off his socks. Surely she wasn't going soft for the man?

She stood, and the only thing between them were the boxers.

Her pussy was moist. Her brain might've screamed one thing, but her womanly parts reacted to his very masculine body. It was a primal, primitive response, one nature had programmed for the success of the species. Giving herself that biology lesson didn't help. Pheromones and knowing he could protect her and defend her honour didn't make her visceral reaction any less irritating.

She put her hand inside his boxers and held his thickness—and God help her, he *was* thick—so that the elastic waistband didn't get caught on his cockhead.

She lowered herself to her knees as she drew his boxers off.

He buried his hands in her hair.

She looked at the size of him.

Dear God, he was magnificent. His ball sac hung heavy. She was unable to resist the impulse of cupping him the way he'd cradled her breasts.

His jutting cock was long and full, and a drop of pre-ejaculate glistened on the top. She'd never fit all of him in her mouth, and she had doubts about her pussy, too, even though that part of her throbbed in mischievous anticipation.

She licked that first drop from his slit.

"Damn," he said.

Revelling in her feminine power, she opened her mouth to accept his cockhead. She placed her tongue on the underside of him and sucked.

He groaned and moved his hips. She curled a hand around his girth so she could control the power of his thrusts. Slowly, oh so slowly, she took more of him.

"You'll be the death of me."

With his hand in her hair and her hand around him, they found a rhythm.

As she pleasured him, she felt her pussy grow moist.

She'd enjoyed giving head before, but never like this. She'd never been so attuned with her partner's responses.

His cock seemed to pulse, and she wondered if she'd got him to climax this quickly.

"You'll take every drop?" he asked.

She mumbled her assent. The words had been a question, more than a demand. And she knew he still had the wherewithal to pull back and stop if she needed him to.

"You're fecking hot, *a rún*."

Then he ceased speaking. The only sounds were the drone from the jet's engines and her working him.

He groaned again, a longer, more sustained sound.

His cock thickened again and his hips jerked forward. He held the back of her skull in place and thrust deeply into her mouth as his seed spilled. She continued to drink from him as his hips jerked and he shuddered.

She remained on her knees as his cock became flaccid.

He slowly relaxed his grip on her head and when he finally let go she sank back on her heels. She looked up and saw his gaze was fixed on her.

His face wasn't soft as she expected, replete from a killer orgasm. Instead, he appeared possessive. He reached out and caught a handful of her hair in a caveman-like way. His woman. He might not have spoken the words aloud, but every part of him silently screamed his possession.

Giving him the slip in downtown Denver had been difficult, but if she thought she'd get away from him again without a fight, she realised she'd been mistaken. Jaysus, God, what the hell was she going to do?

"I'll last longer now when I fuck you."

That hadn't been all he had? Men in her experience didn't recover that quickly. Not that it had happened dozens of times, but when she gave a blowjob, she usually had a couple of hours to herself, either to sleep next to the lazy slug or go compose some music, and sometimes both.

He kept his hand in her hair as he said, "It's no secret, Sinead, that I'm a bit kinky."

"A bit? That's an understatement. Barmy if you ask me."

"And you'll deny you haven't liked it so far?"

"Trying to appease you, oh lord and master."

"And you'll deny the fact you want to be spanked?"

"I'm not a naughty schoolgirl."

"Maybe not a schoolgirl," he allowed, "but naughty for sure. Kneel up," he snapped.

His tone had changed, brooking no disagreement. Her insides tightened in arousal.

"Off your heels."

He kept his hand in her hair and guided her where he wanted her. She knew she could—should—protest, but she didn't.

"Spread your knees farther apart."

That was easier said than done in the tight space. She was somewhat surprised that she followed his orders so completely. But there was something compelling in his voice. And, honestly, she was curious. No man had ever taken her this far. As much as she fought him, she was enjoying him pushing her limits.

"Hands behind your neck," he told her.

She followed his direction.

He nodded.

"Now arch your back and stick out your chest a bit, as if you're offering your breasts to me."

She did as he instructed. Unbelievably she noticed his cock was getting hard again.

"I want you to remember this position," he said. "When I tell you to be in the kneel-up position, this is what I require. Understand?"

She nodded.

"Tell me. Explain it to me."

She licked her lower lip. Her mouth was suddenly dry. "Kneel up means I'm on my knees, my legs spread far apart. Hands behind my head, back arched so my chest sticks out."

"Unless otherwise instructed, keep your gaze downcast."

She immediately looked at the ground.

"Lovely."

She almost, almost glanced up at him.

"If I tell you to kneel back, I want your buttocks resting on your heels like you were earlier. I always want your legs far apart. When you're kneeling back, shoulders rolled forward a bit. It's how I allow you to relax a bit. But that doesn't mean you can be careless. I want you to always remember that if you're kneeling, we're in a scene."

"A scene?"

"You know what BDSM is."

She swallowed deeply.

"Look up at me."

She did. "Yes. In a general way. But I've never experienced it."

His arms were folded across his chest. His legs were spread shoulder-width apart. He looked powerful, large and in charge.

And his cock commanded her attention.

"Tell me what you know or what you think you know."

"One person is a Dom, one a sub."

"Sometimes there can be a person who's a switch. But that doesn't fit here. So, yes, one person is a Dom and one is a sub, unless there are more than two people in a scene. There will be times during a scene with me that you will have me as a Dom along with another man who's a submissive."

"Two?" Was that squeaky sound really her voice? "You'd share me with another man?"

"If I wanted and only with who I wanted."

She reeled. Be involved with two men at the same time? The idea scared her, thrilled her. "You're telling me you also have other submissives?"

"I have a manservant, aye, who fulfils every need."

"A man? Not a woman? But a man?"

"Are you that shockable, *muirnín*? If it's that much of a problem for you, we can discuss it later. But only after you've been involved in a scene."

She blinked up at him.

"Touch your fingers to your cunt!"

Shaking, she complied.

"Hold them up."

He snagged her wrist and lifted her fingers to his nose. Then he sucked the juices from each of her fingers. "You hate the idea, I see."

They both knew the truth. The idea turned her on.

Having her fingers in his mouth was more erotic than she imagined. If he continued to suck like that, she might climax again.

He released her hand. "Continue to finger your pussy. Without coming. What else do you know about BDSM?"

"There's spanking involved."

"There can be," he agreed.

Her stomach was in knots of excitement, of fear, of anticipation. "Whips, chains, bondage, humiliation, gags, hoods, nipple clamps…" She paused. Then, on an exhaled rush, she continued, "I have read about anal sex, plugs, enemas, the like."

He nodded.

She swallowed. "Then there's the obedience and punishment part."

"All of those can be, yes. Not necessarily all of them, but possibly, depending on the people involved and the boundaries negotiated. But more than anything it's commitment and emotional. For many it's a way of life. Some live the lifestyle continually. Others decide to keep it mainly to a timeframe or location, like the bedroom. But there's always caretaking from the Dom for his or her sub."

Like he'd cared for her last night, even if she didn't want it or need it. He'd held her tight, and when she'd woken, she was tucked in, comfortable and warm. The one time she'd shivered, he'd been there, murmuring soothing words and cradling her.

"It can be a rewarding for everyone."

"And, evidently, you're into BDSM?"

"I am."

Her insides flip-flopped.

"I can negotiate certain boundaries. I can negotiate whether a relationship is twenty-four-seven, a lifestyle or a certain scene. But any woman who I'm involved with needs to understand she'll be my submissive."

"And if I don't want to be your woman or your submissive?"

"You're on your knees," he pointed out. "And you haven't told me to go to hell."

"Yet."

"Touché."

"What if I don't want to be involved in a BDSM scene?"

"What are you asking? We're knee-deep in a scene."

She thought about her answer. She didn't want to run away from this. She'd fantasised about a man who wouldn't put up with nonsense from her, one who would give her screaming orgasms, one who would demand things from her that she'd never dreamt existed.

She wouldn't be with Jack long, so she might as well get something exciting from it, something to hold her through Ireland's long, dreary, cold winter nights. "What if it gets too intense?"

"You heard of safe words," he said. "It's a word you'll use if you're too far out of your comfort zone."

She nodded.

"But if we negotiate ahead of time, there are lines I won't cross unless you ask me to. And it's always my responsibility to stay in control to figure out what you need, what you're capable of handling. I will test your limits and your capabilities. Conversely there may be times you think you want more and I will refuse to accommodate you."

She couldn't see *that* happening.

"Mind you, a safe word isn't something to use lightly. And I won't tolerate you using it often, so be careful. And you may not use it to stop a punishment unless the pain is intolerable."

"Intolerable?"

"Your definition may differ from mine," he said drily. "And since I'm responsible for your wellbeing in a scene, we'll generally go with my sense. If you need to slow down, we can. Honestly, how was your spanking last night?"

She felt the heat of embarrassment chase up her face.

"Keep fingering your pussy."

Since he was keeping her on the verge of an orgasm, she could barely think straight. But she tried to answer his question. "I wanted to hate it," she confessed, "but it was hot."

"Was it too much?"

She met his gaze. "No."

"Did you want more?"

"No!"

"So it was well-paced for your first spanking?"

Were they really having this conversation? "Yes."

"And you're ready for more?"

Was she?

"Do you want to be spanked until you come?"

She laughed, albeit nervously. "I seriously doubt I'll come from you spanking me."

"How damp are your fingers?"

She showed him.

"And you think you can't come from me spanking you?"

She didn't answer as his question seemed rhetorical.

"Tell me your safe word."

"*Dearg*," she said. The Irish for the colour red.

"You'll remember that during a scene?"

"Yes."

He nodded. "You're going to experience your second spanking now," he told her. "For failing to ask permission to come."

Her mouth fell open. "But—"

"The rules are not flexible, Sinead. I told you that you need permission each time you come. Each time. Since you're already a bit sore from last night's spanking, you'll really feel this one. On the bed; into the position I instructed."

Her heart thundering, the sound echoing in her ears, she climbed onto the bed. She got on all fours near the edge of the mattress. Slowly, stalling, she kept her knees apart and lowered her forehead and breasts to the bedspread.

Unable to find her voice, she waited for further instruction.

"Using your hands, spread your buttocks so I can have a nice look at your arsehole and your cunt."

Alternately mortified and excited, she did as he ordered.

"You'll finish up the rest of our trip with a plug in that lovely hole of yours."

Her sphincter tightened involuntarily. She knew better than to protest, though.

He stroked her nether lips. His fingers glided across her dampness. Her clit already felt swollen.

"Tell me how many spanks you deserve, Sinead."

Reading about this was one thing, participating was another. "Five. Since I'm still learning."

She wished she could see his face to read his reaction. Had she named a number higher than he anticipated, or was he disappointed in her cowardly answer?

"During a scene, when addressed directly, you'll respond, and you'll call me Sir. Do I make myself clear?"

"Yes, Sir."

"Five it is. Link your hands at your nape. Count each spank aloud."

She took a deep breath and prepared for the blow. She waited and waited. He allowed the time and silence to stretch.

When it came, the breath left her lungs. It blazed across the tender flesh of upper right thigh. "One," she managed, screwing her eyes closed. "Sir."

"Very good."

He landed the second directly on top of the first, searing her skin. "Two, Sir!" At this point, she was nearly done. "I want to use my safe word."

"Really? After two spanks? You took more than that last night."

She didn't break position, and he didn't give her any verbal cues to follow. Instead, he gently stroked her vulva.

Her body, damn it, betrayed her. She was getting aroused. "Continue," she said. "Please."

"This is for the protest." He caught her on the cunt with a flat palm.

She screamed.

But as the pain receded, adrenaline and sexual demand throbbed in her.

He was silent, as if waiting.

Finally she remembered. "Three. Sir."

"You should thank me for that one."

It had blazed her entire feminine area and she should thank him? Never.

He curled a hand into her hair. "That was a demand, Sinead."

"Thank you." Her body felt warm, and she was feeling a bit wanton all of a sudden, aware of her hips thrusting at him, her vagina and anus exposed, her pussy damp from his attention. And it did somehow feel right to express her appreciation.

"How many more?"

"Two, Sir. Two more."

He smacked her left butt cheek. For some reason this one didn't hurt as bad as the others. Was he backing off?

"Four," she said. "I mean four, Sir."

He slid a finger inside her vagina. When it was wet, he pulled it out and probed at her rear entrance. She swayed from side to side, her hips undulating. She'd never had so many conflicting emotions and sensations at the same time.

He stretched her anus a little before removing his finger and delivering the fifth and final spank to her left buttock, on top of the previous one.

"Five, Sir." She exhaled a shaky breath.

"Do you want to come, little sub?"

Shockingly she did. "Please."

She heard him move, then he spread her buttocks. He tongued her from front to back only a few times before she curled her toes and begged for an orgasm.

"You may come," he said. He sucked her clit hard.

Instantly she lost control. She came on a scream.

The moment he left her, she collapsed and rolled onto her side, shattered, spent. "That was hot," she said.

"Glad you didn't stop?"

She looked at him. His cock stuck out, full and ready, despite the fact she'd sucked him off not long ago. Even though she'd just come as well, she wanted his cock inside her. "You'd have made me take them anyway, eventually."

"I would have, aye. And what do you say now?"

A bit shyly she expressed her gratitude. "Thank you."

He opened a drawer and pulled out a towel. He wiped his hand. Then he pulled out a condom and unwrapped it.

He sheathed himself while she watched. For some reason she found watching a man don a condom an incredibly sexy thing. His motions were confident and quick. And she was all but salivating as she watched him handle his cock.

This experience with him astounded her.

After so many men being scared off by her, after Donal telling her that her tastes were odd, that no self-respecting woman would want to do those things, or have those things done to her, being with the Quinn was refreshing. He didn't find her extreme—in fact, he found her tame. In just the short time they'd been together, he'd pushed her boundaries, from watching her masturbate to probing her anally. He hadn't called her boring, but close.

He grabbed lube from a nightstand and placed the bottle on the bed near her.

"I want you on all fours, Sinead. I want to look at your reddened arse. And I want to be able to spank you while I fuck you."

"Yes," she agreed, getting into position. She couldn't believe she was admitting such a thing, couldn't believe it even appealed to her.

He placed his hands on her hips and drew her back towards him. "Parts of your arse are red," he said. "But not your entire skin. Next time, when you're more brave, when you say you'll take as many as I want to give you, when you trust that I'll give you a punishment that makes you come again and again, both your buttocks will be reddened. Imagine how sex will feel then, Sinead. Imagine."

She felt his cockhead at the entrance to her vagina.

"I'll set the pace," he informed her.

She could have screamed. She just wanted him hard and fast.

He entered her with maddening slowness. He gave her time to accommodate his length and girth. "Down and dirty," she said, trying not to sound as frustrated as she felt. "Please."

He smacked her smartly on her right hip.

And that only made her hungrier.

Even though he'd told her he wanted to set the pace, she thrust her hips backward.

"Demanding sub, aren't you? Do you understand rules?"

"Do you understand that I'm hot for you, Sir?"

Those must have been the right words because he started to move the way she wanted him to. He drove his cock in deeper, impaling her on its length. "Permission to come, Sir?"

"Because you're trying to top from the bottom, forgetting who's the Dom, no. Hold it."

She breathed deep. She tightened her hands together and pulled strands of her own hair as a distraction.

He pounded her relentlessly.

He continually smacked her right flank, not hard, but with enough force to mark her, to sting, to make her even crazier with need.

"Sir!"

"Hold it," he instructed. He smacked her harder.

She tossed her head from side to side.

"Come," he commanded. He pulled out and drove forward with his entire power.

She cried out his name as the orgasm pulsed through her, her pussy muscles contracting around his big cock. Her face was buried in the mattress and she couldn't draw a deep breath.

Her pussy was so full, her right hip burned from his slaps. Honestly she'd never had an orgasm like that before, as if drawn from the deepest parts of her.

He traced her spine with his fingertips. "How are you doing?"

"Never better," she confessed. "Wanting you to come."

"You can put your hands where you want them," he told her. "But I want you to bend your knees, more like you're supporting your weight on your thighs. Keep your legs together. Now lean forward, your forehead on the mattress like before."

With his hands on her waist he pulled her back a bit and guided her into position. "You must have seen this in a book," she said. "One I haven't read."

He was silent, but she felt him against her entrance again. She stretched her hands in front of her, across the mattress. She grabbed hold of the bedspread when she realised what he was about.

The position was more or less a modified squat, so that would make her passageway a bit smaller, probably tighter.

He eased his fat cockhead inside her. She heard him open the bottle of lube. She froze.

"Trust me. "We're not going to do anything we haven't already done."

"That means that massive thing isn't going in my bowels?"

"Crude," he said. "And no, I've no intention of shoving my cock in yer arse. Today."

She shuddered.

"Breathe, little sub."

"I think you're too big for me this way."

"I think you'll like it."

He pulled back then eased forward a couple of times. She heard the lube squirt, then felt his finger at her rear.

It was so exquisitely painful that it was total pleasure.

He pressed his thumb forward as he thrust his cock into her.

She drew in a few breaths. She forced herself to uncurl her hands so she would relax more.

He found a gentle rhythm, easing in a bit, pulling back. Going forward, then going back.

"Bear down," he told her.

Closing her eyes, she did. He penetrated her arse and her pussy completely, simultaneously.

She nearly exploded. His cock was jutting against her G-spot, and it felt as if there were no room. She was completely full of her Dom. "Oh God. Oh God, oh God!"

"You can come any time," he told her.

She didn't need any further encouragement. The slide of his steely, silky cock against her insides undid her. Panting, she came.

He grabbed her by the shoulders, pulling her back a bit as he continued to take her hard.

"I...I'm going to come again."

"Do."

His permission, his command was all she needed. She climaxed a second time, her body shuddering with the force. Seconds later, his body went rigid.

"Damn." The word sounded like a curse as well as an exclamation.

He ejaculated, thrusting into her, holding her imprisoned.

He remained behind her for long moments. Sweat cooled on her back, and he continued to hold her as if she were a cherished lover rather than a lifelong enemy.

It would be so easy to succumb to that. It had been so long since she'd had any affection in her life. And she'd never had it after this kind of passionate sex.

He leaned over and kissed her nape.

"Stay there." He withdrew his cock from her slowly.

A part of her wondered how long she had to wait until they could do it again. The more rational part of her brain warned that she was getting in too deep with this man.

She was tempted to get up and dress, but she was also mindful of her sore arse that was a result of disobeying him.

Still she turned her head to watch what he was doing.

He discarded the condom and took a small metal plug from the still-open dresser drawer. Oh no. She clenched her buttocks in silent protest.

"Up on all fours," he instructed. "Spread your knees as far apart as you can and arch your back so your rear sticks up."

It would be completely obscene, just like he preferred. The man was carnal.

"Lovely," he said when she got into position, confirming her thoughts.

She'd never been with a man who appreciated a woman's private area so much. Most men were interested in sex. She'd had the occasional hot pussy-licking, but this man was a connoisseur of a woman's privates.

"Now relax," he encouraged, returning to her and grabbing the bottle of lube.

"Easy for you to say." More than ever she wanted to run.

"This is a smallish one," he told her, showing her the teardrop-shaped plug. "It's a beginner's size."

A beginner's size? Surely he'd never try to put something bigger than that up there. Lord protect her, she never wanted to see the intermediate or advanced sizes.

He brought the plug closer. "We're skipping some of the others that are for training, because this one is lovely.

It's stainless steel. One of these days we can play with inserting it after I've stuck it in ice water. A whole new sensation."

Her gut contracted just from the threat.

"See the base?"

She blinked. The base was made up of tens of tiny pink crystals, winking in the light. "At the thickest part, this plug is thicker than my finger. I've already stretched your anus a bit, so it won't be a big struggle for you to take it. I'll work it in and out," he explained, "until we get it all the way in. We'll both need a bit of patience, I imagine, for the first time."

The plane hit a tiny amount of turbulence, nothing that didn't happen a dozen times during a typical flight, but it served to make her stomach roil even more.

He cupped the plug in his hand. "I'm warming it a bit," he explained, "so it's not quite a shock to your insides."

She swallowed deeply and watched, mesmerised, as he squirted lube onto the plug, taking care that the entire surface was covered. "Push back against it," he instructed.

She felt the cool wetness at her anus. She wanted to protest that she couldn't do it. But she wanted to take it, oddly, because it would please him.

With his left hand he grasped her left hipbone, holding her steady. "It will only take a few tries, pushing it in, pulling it out, stretching that sphincter muscle as we go. If you struggle, *muirnín*, it will be a much nastier experience."

How many different endearments did he know? And why did she like hearing them so much. "Hard to imagine how it could be a nastier experience." She forced herself to breathe, in and out, instead of shallow little pants of panic.

"Work with me."

She nodded against the bedspread.

"Keep your body in position. Bear down. Try to relax."

"Yes," she whispered. Really, for all her fuss, the plug wasn't that big. And it was lovely. She'd seen pictures online of big thick silicone ones. They weren't beautiful, like this one. And others were longer, which she knew would be considerably more uncomfortable when she tried to sit.

She promised herself she'd stay in position. Having his finger up her hole hadn't been as bad as she feared. In fact, she had found the experience added to her sexual pleasure.

But as the unyielding firmness pressed against her tightest space, she pitched her hips forward.

"Steady yourself," he encouraged her.

She had expected his displeasure, but his soft words encouraged her to just lie there.

"Back into position, sub."

When she didn't return to his ordered position, he released his grip on her and delivered a smart smack to her buttock.

"I gave you a command."

Her eyes filled with tears, she spread her knees apart, arched her back and put her head on the bedspread.

"Reach back," he told her. "I've decided I want you more involved. I want you holding your buttocks apart for me."

She could safe word out. And for a moment, she was tempted. But really, she told herself, wasn't the experience worth it? She'd read stories where the Dom had insisted his sub wear a plug and she'd wondered what that felt like.

Slowly and reluctantly, she reached back and spread her cheeks.

"Makes me want to shove my cock in there."

"You'd tear me apart."

He laughed. "Shall we see?"

That threat made her decide not to protest the plug. At this point, she was a bit unsure of him. Would he really try that? Now? "Please, Sir, put the plug in my arse." Anything to avoid the *other*.

"Lord, woman, you're perfect."

And he wasn't focussed on that big dick of his going up there.

He gently eased the tip of the plug in and pulled it back out several times.

"Aye, that's a good sub."

Each time, it went a bit deeper, and the stupid plug got a bit thicker.

"Keep breathing, Sinead. Work with me."

She felt the bigger part of the plug forcing that tight muscle apart.

He pushed firmly. With a barely audible pop, the plug sank home.

She gasped.

"Give it a few seconds. The worst is over."

The hilt of the plug was surprisingly small, and her sphincter muscle snuggled around it to hold the metal in place.

Within a few seconds, the pain went away almost entirely. Getting the plug in was a challenge, but now that it was there, it wasn't all that terrible.

"You look beautiful with your arsehole stuffed full just for me."

She shuddered. The feeling was alien, completely different from having his finger slide in and out during the heat of intercourse. This was a relentless reminder that she was obeying his orders, that he'd declared himself the Dom and she his sub...and that she'd followed along happily.

He went into the small bathroom just off to the side of the bedroom. All the comforts, she realised.

When he returned, he had a damp flannel. Like she was coming to expect, he cleaned her then patted her dry with a second towel.

There was something soothing about this routine. It made her feel cared for.

"You did well," he told her gently, turning her so that she lay on her back looking up at him.

His approval did strange things to her emotionally. It shouldn't matter at all. But it did. It made the spanks a badge of honour, it made the nasty plug tolerable.

"You pleased me."

She wondered, just for a moment, what things might be like if he weren't a Quinn. What if he were simply a man from back home? What if her family wouldn't be shocked and appalled if she brought him home?

"I'll look forward to the rest of the trip knowing you're wearing my plug."

"I'm not sure I want to sit on the damn thing."

He grinned.

He suddenly looked younger, boyishly cheeky. He'd see her discomfort and enjoy it because she suffered for him.

"You should have a look in the mirror," he told her. "Bend over, spread your legs, and have a look at how sexy it is. See yourself as I see you."

He helped her from the bed and he held onto her as she manoeuvred into position.

The pretty pink crystals sparkled in the overhead light. He was right. It looked pretty and feminine. Even if it felt like a beast.

"Beautiful," he told her. "Absolutely beautiful."

As he watched, arms folded across his chest, she got dressed again.

They returned to their seats.

"Something to drink?" Aonghus asked.

She felt a bit embarrassed, wondering if the man realised what they'd been about. But Aonghus behaved as if Jack and his female guest disappearing to the back of the aircraft were a common enough occurrence.

Maybe it was.

That thought made her scowl.

"Scotch," Jack said. "Neat."

What did she really know about the man who'd just claimed her? Mayhap he had a woman with him on every flight.

Now that they were in their seats, the thrill of the orgasm wore off and her sanity returned. What was she doing, being perfectly responsive to a Quinn, behaving with wanton abandon, wearing his plug and asking for more? Had she lost her mind? "Red wine, if you have it." Maybe it would help take the edge off and she could doze. She needed to be rested and have her wits about her as soon as they made it to Ireland.

Chapter Six

Sinead O'Malley had been worth the wait. He could have taken her in her Denver hotel room. But her orgasms and his enforced wait had made it all the better.

Her repeated rejections had only served to whet his appetite. And now, knowing how she responded sensually to his dominating commands had hooked him. He looked forward to guiding her down the path to total surrender. And wouldn't it be glorious when she wriggled her arse and begged for his lash?

He pulled the sports utility vehicle to a stop in front of the iron gates. He lowered the window and punched in the numeric code for admittance. From his spot behind the steering wheel, he glanced over at her.

She was leaned up against the passenger window, as far away from him as the SUV's interior allowed.

She'd pulled away from him mentally, emotionally, physically after the scene in the jet. As soon as he had her alone, they could address it. "Welcome home."

"To Ireland, aye," she allowed, looking at him. "But Quinn Manor is your home. Not mine. Never mine. And you'll do well to remember that."

"Does everything have to be a fight, *a rún*? Everything?"

The gates swung wide, and he drove through. The vehicle's headlamps illuminated the trees and flowers. He'd left the window down so he could inhale the fresh, crisp air, so different than the cities he'd been in recently.

There was something about returning home that always soothed his battered soul, no matter how short a time he'd been gone.

He followed the curved driveway around and braked to a stop in front of the stone steps, steps that had been in place since Columbus discovered the Americas.

The house hadn't stood quite as long. Family legend had it that the original structure had been destroyed in some clan fighting in the early sixteenth century. The Quinns, known for their resilience, had rebuilt.

In the darkest hours before dawn, he cut the vehicle's engine and turned off the headlamps.

He opened his door, then climbed out of the car. He drank in the richness and the dampness of the night air. His roots ran deep. He came around to her side of the vehicle. "There's no place I'd rather be. "I hope, in time, you'll feel the same."

Liam, who was at least one hundred years old, or so it seemed, welcomed them, with lights blazing.

"Back to bed with you," Jack said to the man who was more friend than servant. "No need for you to have been disturbed."

"Your grandmother would've skinned me alive if I hadn't met you. I'm terrified of the woman, Sir. She told me Mistress Sinead was to be warmly welcomed no matter the time of day or night."

He grinned. He knew a story when he heard one. Aye, his grandmother wanted Sinead to feel welcomed, but she would have never threatened Liam. She was as fond of the man as she was her grandson. Truth was, Liam was as nosy as the day was long. Having had first glimpse of Sinead, he'd be popular amongst the other gossiping employees. "Right then. Liam, I'd like you to meet Sinead O'Malley. Sinead, the man who keeps the estate, even the family, running, Liam Doyle."

The man's bushy grey eyebrows drew together to form a thick, single line. "My pleasure."

He bowed so deeply that Jack wondered how the man would ever stand up straight again.

"A pleasure to meet you, Liam. For the short time until I return to my own family, I appreciate your hospitality."

Had Jack actually thought any part of this would be easy?

She turned to him and smiled. Smiled. Her entire face lit up, especially when she defied him.

He trailed his hand down her spine. As she stood there frozen, he continued lower. He grabbed a handful of her right butt cheek through her jeans and squeezed tightly in silent warning.

She gasped and stood up a bit straighter.

"Trouble, Sir?" Liam asked.

"Indeed no."

Sinead, to her credit, dealt with her own bag rather than allow Liam to handle it. Jack appreciated her thoughtfulness. Perhaps he'd reward her for it later.

"Upstairs with you," Jack ordered.

"Nice to know you," she said to Liam as the man showed them inside and closed the massive wooden door behind them.

Jack took her bag from her.

"I can manage," she protested.

"Aye. That you can. But when you're with me, I'll thank you to let me be the man."

"Even if you have your own luggage to deal with?"

"Even then," he agreed.

"Good night, Sir. Welcome to Quinn Manor, ma'am," Liam threw the bolt home.

As they headed up the stairs, she said to Jack, "Servants? In this day and age? Aren't you the lord of the manor?"

Good thing her words weren't arrows. "And now your lord and Master."

She stopped on the stairs and turned to look at him.

"I've noticed that you tend to be much more willing and compliant when you're naked," he said. "I may keep you that way, sub."

Liam coughed discreetly.

She had the grace to blush.

"To my rooms," he instructed.

At the top of the stairs, she stepped aside. He led the way down the hall, then stopped in front of the door to his suite. After juggling the luggage, he opened the door. When she just stood there, he nudged her. "After you, my lady."

"My lady? As if I'm anything other than a pawn."

"After you, my pawn." This time, he shoved her into the room.

He closed the door behind them. He dropped the keys on a small table just inside the doorway. Then he shrugged from his jacket and draped it over the newel bed post. "We'll catch a couple of hours sleep before we join *máthair Chríona* for breakfast. I wouldn't mind fucking you first, however." Just the small amount of their verbal sparring had left him with a raging hard-on.

"Thanks, but I'd rather sleep."

She had a whole lot to learn about being his submissive. He regarded her. She still wore that cheeky T-shirt, but the fact his plug was still shoved up her arse made him smile. He should keep her full up.

He moved into an oversized closet and left the door open. He pulled off his shirt and dropped it to the carpeted floor.

"You know, I meant to comment earlier. But for an older guy, you're not half bad."

"Older?" he asked, sticking out his head and looking at her. "Older than you by how much? Five years? Six?"

Sinead stood there, unabashedly staring at him. She frowned, as if in deep concentration. "At least five. But you may want to take a look at adding a few more reps when you work out."

"You really know how to make an old guy feel good." He unfastened his belt and wrapped the length around his hand. He considered using the leather on her fair backside. If she were still red from the earlier spanking, she'd feel the next much more keenly.

"No you don't," she said as if reading his mind.

"Don't tempt me." He slipped out of his shoes and took off his socks.

She unzipped her luggage and pulled out fresh knickers.

Lord, he preferred her in nothing at all. Feeling as if the temperature were suddenly several degrees warmer he re-entered the closet.

Even though he'd got off twice on the jet, his cock was hardening again. The idea of the strap across her bare buttocks morphed into a fantasy of pulling out the plug and stuffing a larger one up her hole before letting her go to sleep.

By the time he unbuttoned his khakis and dropped them, his dick was fully erect.

He reached for a dressing gown then discarded the idea. He was going to fuck Sinead. Why bother with clothes?

When he re-entered the bedroom, she was nowhere to be found.

Cursing in two languages, he opened the door and headed down the stairs, naked as the day he was born.

As the front door was locked, it was clear Liam was much cleverer than Jack. She slid open the lock and was tugging the door open when Jack came up behind her and slammed the door closed.

She yelped and jumped.

Calmly he placed a hand alongside her head. Deliberately he moved closer, pressing her belly against the door. He'd lost his erection during his dash down the stairs, but now that he was against her rear, his cock was thickening again. He held her trapped, immobile. Her breathing was ragged, and her shoulders shook slightly. He wondered if she was as turned on as he was. Were they two of a kind? Against her ear, he whispered, "Enough."

She stilled. "I'll not stop fighting you."

"And I'll see you do." Jack captured her right hand and raised it high, pinning it to the door.

"Release me, you bastard."

"When you give your word you'll walk up the stairs to my room. Or we can stay here all night long. I'm not sure how much longer I will be able to restrain myself." He nipped at the top of her ear then soothed the tiny insult with the tip of his tongue. "Do you know what I'm thinking just now? I'm thinking I'll just pull out your butt plug right here and take you against the door. What do you think, Sinead? Shall I take you right here in the entrance of Quinn Manor?"

"Please…"

"Say it, Sinead. Say you surrender."

"For now."

He laughed. "Not good enough. What'll it be? Your total surrender? Or shall I fuck your arse right here, right now?"

"I surrender," she whispered.

He ground his cock against her and simulated the sex act, bending his knees, driving upwards a little.

"Stop!"

"Say it."

"Right. Yes…"

He thrust against her rear.

"I surrender."

"Say it like you mean it."

"I surrender," she whispered, sounding somewhat defeated.

"I surrender, Sir," he prompted.

"I surrender, Sir."

This time, her words had a breathless quality that turned him on even more. "That's my lass."

"In your dreams."

This time, he took no chances. He released her right hand and took a step back. "Strip."

"I beg your pardon?"

He folded his arms across his chest.

"Here?" she whispered, looking above his head to the top of the stairs.

"Here," he confirmed. "Now."

She swallowed. "Your grandmother…"

"My grandmother is upstairs in her bedroom. If you continue making a racket, she'll wake up and come to see what all the fuss is about. If you don't want her seeing you naked, you might want to shut up and follow my orders."

"What about your servant?"

"He was married." Sometime in the past hundred years. "You've nothing he hasn't seen before. I'll have you naked now, if you please."

"You're a beast."

"Indeed." A beast with a cock that throbbed demandingly.

With a glance at the stairs, she pulled off her T-shirt.

"Drop it on the floor."

She opened her mouth as if to protest. When he glared, she lowered her gaze and released the cotton shirt. "Now the bra."

"Honestly! You've made your point."

"The bra."

She reached behind her and unhooked the material.

"Drop it."

She did.

He ached to feel the fullness of her breasts in his palms, wanted to tease those nipples into even harder firmness. "You really are lovely with your nipples erect like that."

"Someone will hear you," she whispered furiously.

"Take off your shoes."

She glared, but she stepped out of her sandals.

"And the rest, if you please."

Her chin was set mutinously, but she followed his order and removed her jeans and thong.

Her bush was neatly trimmed and he smelt the scent of her heat. She was all woman. *His* woman. He'd had his hands off her for hours, and it turned out that was longer than he could tolerate.

Jack couldn't help himself. He knelt, right there in his family home's historic entry way. He reached around her, pressing one palm against her warm buttocks and another against the small of her back. His arousal grabbed him hard and fast. He wanted this woman. Nothing to do with the past, with revenge. Everything to do with raw, animalistic need. His pulse quickened.

He pressed his mouth against her hot mound. "Spread your legs."

"What? Here? Are you mad?"

"Completely. Now spread your legs." When she hesitated, he slapped her cunt.

With a gasp, she parted her legs.

Despite her verbal protests, his Sinead was hot and ready. Her pussy was moist, making his cock pulse.

He pushed on the plug slightly. Her hips jerked forward and she dug her hands into his hair. "You're a hot woman." He licked her clit. When she moaned, he sucked on it slightly. Then he tongued inside her vagina.

He felt her pussy muscles clench, spasming in advance of her orgasm.

There was nothing he wanted more than to feel her come around his tongue. But she was also at her most vulnerable in this moment. Reluctantly he stopped tasting her. "Upstairs with you," he said.

He stood and moved away from her.

Groggily she blinked.

He gently tugged.

"You really are a scoundrel."

With his hands on her shoulders, he moved her away from the door and towards the stairs. She didn't argue. Perhaps she was finally learning that he didn't make idle threats.

He stayed a step below her on the way up the stairs. Customarily he preferred his subs to follow him at a respectful distance. This one wasn't trained well enough to do that yet. Besides, this way, he got to watch the way her arse swayed, and he caught an occasional glimpse of the bling between her buttocks.

In his suite, he closed the door and locked it behind them. He dropped the key into a drawer. It wouldn't necessarily stop her from bolting, but it would certainly slow her down. "I may always keep you naked, *a rún*."

"I prefer to sleep in a T-shirt."

"Indeed?"

"One of yours is fine."

"Generous of you. Into bed." He opened another drawer and pulled out a pair of soft leather cuffs.

As she climbed onto the bed, she kept a wary eye on him. "What are you about?" she asked. She sat on the mattress and pulled her legs protectively to her chest. She wrapped her arms around her legs.

Jack moved fast. He crossed the room, grabbed her. Within seconds and despite her struggles he secured her to the bedpost.

"Release me this instant."

He folded his arms across his chest and regarded the squirming, sexy wee bit of woman on his bed. Loveliness and a hellion rolled into one. The ensuing years may be a lot of different things, but boring would never be among them.

"This is an outrage. Despite what you think, we've moved on from the Middle Ages. You cannot kidnap me and keep me against my will."

"My lady, it appears I already have."

He left her there on the bed, beautiful in her anger.

"Damn you," she said. "No! No, no, no! Damn you! Let me out of this bloody thing!"

He regarded her.

She appeared pissed, but not panicked, angry that he'd bested her, perhaps furious that he'd denied her an orgasm.

There was a knock on his door.

He went to answer it.

"You can't just leave me here, Quinn."

"Aye, until you learn some manners, I certainly can." He pulled on a pair of jogging pants. The material did nothing to disguise the size of his erection.

He unlocked the door to find Liam there.

"Mistress Sinead appears to have left her clothing in the foyer, sir."

Sinead groaned audibly.

Liam raised his bushy brows. "May I suggest a gag, sir?" Liam handed over the pile of clothes. "I've found a gag plenty handy. Unless you have use of her mouth for other purposes."

Jack blinked, for once in his life dumbfounded.

Liam nodded sagely and shuffled off.

"I shall drown in mortification," Sinead told him, when he closed the door.

"I'm not certain I won't," he admitted. He placed her clothes on top of his wardrobe. "Now, where were we?"

"You were deciding not to be a beast."

"I was deciding whether or not to strap your legs to the footboard."

"I'm not into bondage."

"Really?" He sat on the edge of the bed. He leaned over, and he pinned her thighs to the mattress with his torso. "Is that why your pussy is all but dripping?" He feathered a finger between the folds of her vulva. "Because you're not into bondage? Or is it because you don't like being naked in the entryway? Or maybe because you're hoping I take pity on you and take out that plug."

She ceased her struggles. In silent surrender, she arched her back and dug her heels into the mattress.

"Jack! Please!"

"Please what? Please stop? Please order me to spread my legs? Please lick my clit? Please suck on it? Please touch it? Please give me the screaming orgasm you denied me downstairs?"

"Yes!"

"Which?"

"All of them…"

He moved aside and she opened her legs wide.

"Tell me what you want." He moved between her legs, facedown. After parting her folds, he laved his tongue across the sensitive, already-swollen little nub. He worked his tongue against her with a little more pressure. "Ask for it. Be specific. Be graphic. Beg me. Call me your master."

She shook her head. But he knew it was only a matter of time, both in the bedroom and out of it. "I love having my face in your pussy. I like the way you taste. I love how moist you are. I like how responsive."

Her free hand was in his hair. She wasn't pulling, instead, she was holding on, keeping him in place.

"Tell me," he said against her heated skin.

"I..."

"The bondage you keep yourself in, Sinead, is more powerful than the bonds that confine you. Be honest, Sinead. Be honest with me. More importantly, with yourself. I'll give you one last chance. Tell me what you want, else I'll leave the plug in and just let us both go to sleep."

"Heathen!"

He rolled off her. By tomorrow, if he knew women, she'd be following him, crawling after him, begging for what she wanted, what she would realise she needed.

"Please, Jack."

"You're trying my patience."

"I want you to lick me."

He sat on the edge of the bed and captured her chin with his thumb and forefinger. "That's a start. I want you to be graphic."

She swallowed. "I want you to lick my pussy."

"More graphic," he snapped.

"Lick my cunt," she pleaded.

Jaysus. He wasn't sure his cock could take this. He wasn't sure *he* could take it. "And then?"

"Suck my clit. When I'm about to come, gently bite it."

"There now. Just add some manners and a little begging and you'll get what you want."

She scowled. "That wasn't good enough?"

"I want you to know you're mine. "I want you to beg prettily. I want your honesty." He fingered her, bringing her to arousal again. "Do you like that?"

"Yes," she whispered.

He felt her entire body tremble.

"Please lick my cunt, Sir."

As he did what she asked, she continued, "Please, please bring me off. Please, I beg you!" She writhed. "I want you. I need you. I need this."

She pulled against the restraint. She moaned. She continued to beg prettily.

God help him if she ever discovered the truth, that she held tremendously more power over him than he'd ever hold over her.

Her eyes closed. With her free hand, she held his head while she slowly rotated her hips. Could she be any more spectacular?

"Sir...?"

She was only seconds away, there was no doubt.

"Sir..."

This time he shuddered. The word sounded sweet on her lovely lips.

"Fuck me," she demanded. "I want your cock in my cunt."

In that instant she could have asked for a star for her neck and he would have figured out how to have it boxed and wrapped.

He left her for a moment and took off the jogging pants before grabbing a condom from a drawer.

He returned to her, feeling simultaneously predatory and protective. An enemy for eight hundred years, she was tied to his bedpost. Maybe if an ancestor of his had done this centuries ago, there'd have been peace across the land.

"Fuck me hard, Sir."

Despite her respectful words, there was no doubting the command in her voice. The O'Malley lass wasn't a perfect little submissive but she was the perfect woman for him.

He took her with no preliminaries, sinking deep into her with a single thrust.

"Yes," she said. "More. Harder. Deeper. Please, Sir."

Her hot pussy clenched around him, milking his balls.

She clenched her free hand onto his shoulder. "Sir, please. I need to come."

"Wait," he told her. She'd asked permission. That should have been enough for him, but it wasn't. He was delaying his satisfaction. She could, as well. He slowed his thrusts and made each a little more shallow.

She dug her fingernails into his skin.

"It'll be sweeter for the waiting."

"Sir…"

He didn't respond, but he captured her left nipple and squeezed it brutally.

She bucked and gasped.

"Now?" she demanded. "Please!"

"Exquisite," he told her. "*Now.*

"I can come?"

"Yes." He filled her, pulled back then pressed forward again. He worked a hand beneath her hips and tilted the angle of her pelvis so as to rub her G-spot with each stroke.

"Saints," she whispered.

"Come," he whispered, urged, demanded. He increased the tempo of his movements.

Seconds later, her internal muscles tightened.

"Yes."

She arched her back and screamed his surname as she shattered.

The force of her climax drove his, and Jack could hold out no longer. He grabbed hold of her hips, imprisoning her.

"Fill me," she said against his ear.

She didn't submit as any other woman had. But her lusty demands were more satisfying than her quiet capitulation would have been.

He groaned as the first spurt of semen pulsed into her heat.

Her fingers curled into his shoulder. His body jerked as a second spasm claimed him and pleasure spilled from him. There was something about this woman...

He supported his weight with his elbows. He kissed, licked, nipped the exposed side of her neck. He was never glad of bloodshed, would never have wanted it. And maybe his grandmother was right—'twas time the two of them ended the feud.

"This doesn't mean I'll marry you or stop fighting you," she said, as if reading his mind.

He sighed. "A truce?" he asked, rising up slightly and supporting his weight on his palms. He looked down at her. Her lips were slightly opened and her breaths were a bit shallow. If it weren't for her narrowed eyes, she'd look like a happy, sated woman.

"I'll thank you to release me so I can take out your unwelcomed plug. I need some sleep and you're interfering with it."

Ah. Had he expected any of this to be easy? "I'll remove it for you."

"Absolutely not!"

"In that case, I'll accompany you to the toilet."

"I beg your pardon?"

"You've denied me a truce. You've tried several escapes. You've not earned trust or privacy."

"I'll not allow you in the toilet with me."

"In that case…" He moved off the bed and discarded the condom in the rubbish. He grabbed a couple of flannels from the linen closet and dampened them with warm water. When he returned, he told her, "Open your legs."

"I can do this myself."

"No doubt. Now spread your legs else I'll lash them to the bedposts."

"You—"

"Yes, I would dare. And I'll leave you tied the rest of the night unless you cease your struggles. Your choice, Sinead. Spread your legs and raise your knees to your chest within three seconds or we'll do it my way."

He placed the washcloths on a nightstand. He was resolute. His way or his way.

She opened her mouth as if to protest then she closed it again.

With her own form of defiance, she followed orders, but she took more than the allotted three seconds.

For that, she'd be oh-so-tantalisingly punished.

"Have you ever been blindfolded while being explored? Do you know what it's like to be forced to depend on all your other senses?"

"No," she whispered.

Her breathing changed. Her chest rose and fell in quick succession.

Even though he'd just had her, he wanted her again. His dick had never become completely flaccid and it was thickening again.

He grabbed a blindfold from the nightstand. "Straighten your head," he told her when she turned to the left.

Without protest, maybe curious despite herself, she looked up at him, unblinking as he lowered the blindfold.

She moaned slightly but didn't protest when he laid the black material across her eyes and lifted her head to secure the straps in place.

"I want you to listen to me," he said quietly.

Instinctively she turned her head the direction of his voice.

"You won't know what I'm going to do next." He tweaked one of her nipples and she whimpered.

"You won't know if I'm going to remove the plug gently or if I'm going to yank it out." He stroked the inside of her right thigh but didn't touch her intimately. "Keep your knees up, your legs apart."

She clenched her buttocks. Obviously, since he'd planned it that way, she expected him to tug on the butt plug.

Instead he manoeuvred quietly to cup her right breast as if weighing it, then as she relaxed, he moved. Before she could possibly know what he was about, he pulled back the hood covering her clit and sucked hard on the distended nub.

She screamed.

She was passionate and responsive, and part of him hoped she continued to deny him a truce. He took her free hand and fastened it to the headboard. She was totally exposed and vulnerable, spread apart and opened. "Now you're deprived of touch. "She could release her left hand at any time, but she didn't. She was as attuned to this pleasure as he was.

Lightly, he slapped her hot cunt.

She arched. She screamed.

He slapped her again.

She drank in a huge gulp of air.

He shoved three fingers deep inside her wet pussy.

"Feck!"

That wasn't at all ladylike. And wasn't that what he wanted? His smile was triumphant, and he was as delighted for her as he was for himself.

He finger-fucked her, with long, slow thrusts, then shorter, faster ones. She writhed and thrashed.

Then he kissed her mouth.

She responded ferociously, biting and sucking.

He shoved a hand into her hair and pulled.

He swallowed her cry with a deeply brutal kiss. He felt her tongue in his mouth, meeting each of his demands with one of her own.

He ended the kiss and returned his mouth to her pussy, lapping up the juices, and causing a wave of fresh ones.

He brought her to the edge and kept her teetering there. He grabbed hold of the base of the plug. As he tongued her and sucked her, he eased the plug in and pulled it just back to the point her sphincter resisted. He wanted her familiar with the sensation, comfortable with his exploration of her anus.

She dug her heels into the mattress and arched her hips towards him, offering her entire body with tiny whimpers. Then, just then, he increased the pressure and motions of his tongue and simultaneously yanked out the butt plug.

She yelped and cursed. "I—"

"Give me your orgasm," he demanded. "Now." He continued to manipulate her with his fingers for only a couple more seconds until her climax overtook her.

"Good God," she said. Her chest rose and fell, her ribcage expanding and contracting furiously.

Oh yes, she was perfect in her response. And their descent into BDSM would be a fast and furious one.

"Your arse is stretched." He looked at her, admiring her, wanting her. "I think you'll like it when I fuck you up there," he said. "Or when Logan fills your arse while I claim that hot pussy of yours."

She shivered, but he couldn't tell whether it was from fear or excitement or a combination of the two.

"You're joking about sharing me with another man."

"A man of my choosing," he clarified. "I'll not be a cuckold. But within the confines of a scene I set up, aye."

He left her long enough to dampen a flannel and rinse the plug.

When he returned, he removed the blindfold then gently cleansed her.

It'd been years since he'd had a woman in his bed. Usually he booked a hotel or slept at her place. He rarely spent an entire night with any woman. He certainly didn't snuggle of his own choice.

He pulled up the blankets and covered her naked shoulders.

"Are you going to leave me naked and bound?" she demanded.

"Indeed I am. I want a peaceful night's sleep."

"If I can't turn over or if I'm cold I won't be having a peaceful night."

"More's the pity."

"You're seriously going to treat me like a captive and keep—"

"Sub," he interrupted, turning onto his side and gathering her close. He shaped his body to hers and placed an arm across her torso. His partially aroused cock bumped against her lovely behind.

"Semantics."

"Cease your struggles," he told her. "If you were a proper sub, you'd happily go along with my wishes because they're my wishes."

"Not a chance."

"And that's why you'll be kept naked and confined for the rest of the night."

"Beast," she said, but the word lacked real heat. She kept her body rigid for a few moments before slowly relaxing.

He smiled against her hair. So, this was what peace felt like with this woman. He decided to enjoy it, knowing it wouldn't last long.

Chapter Seven

"Top of the morning, Mistress O'Malley."

No one actually said that anymore. Not sincerely. So that meant Sinead was having a nightmare, a living, nasty, vicious nightmare. And Quinn was the centre of it all.

"Wake up, vixen. *Móraí* would like to meet you."

His grandmother wanted to meet her?

Sinead blinked against the grit in her eyes. Her head ached and her confined arm had grown numb.

The memory of last night flooded back. On its wings were an illicit thrill and a sense of shame from being out of control, for asking him to do unspeakable things to her. No one, anywhere, anytime, had got the response from her that her mortal enemy had. She hated that.

And damn it, she hated that he looked so devastatingly handsome.

He wore a long-sleeved black T-shirt and a pair of trousers that accented his firm buttocks. The black suited him perfectly, with his dark Irish looks and lord of the manor attitude. "Unfasten me so that I can choke you."

"You truly are a ray of sunshine in the mornings."

"Does *téigh transa ort féin* mean anything to you?"

"I'll take *go fuck yourself* as an invitation to join you in bed and sample a few more of your delicacies? I have not, for example, put nipple clamps on you." He shot a glance towards a partially open drawer.

It was the one, she presumed, where he'd found the butt plug last night.

Seemingly unperturbed by her behaviour or the fact he still had her tied to the bedpost, he stood near the bed and sipped deeply from a stout mug.

"Coffee?" she asked. Her eyes narrowed as she looked at him. "Is that coffee? Not tea?"

"Coffee. American. Hot." He took a drink. "Strong. A splash of cream, a couple of spoons of sugar. It's prepared just the way you like it, if I recall."

Despite herself, her mouth moistened.

Damn it, it wasn't just from the idea of coffee. It was from him. He stood there, a thick Aran sweater emphasising the breadth of his shoulders. She was mesmerised by him, his dark eyes, the hypnotic shape of his lips, the firm, square shape of his chin.

She was all-too-aware of her nakedness and the way she'd so wantonly submitted to him. But it had been more than simple submission.

Sinead turned her head to the side, looking away from him, trying to gather her wits.

She'd been vulnerable and needy.

She'd wanted his possession.

Everything he'd given her had made her hungry for more.

Who knew all that had been in her? Who knew her hated enemy was the one man to bring it to the surface, to make her scream out an orgasm and beg for more? "There's more?" she asked.

He took a few moments answering. Over the mug's rim, he casually mentioned, "There's a full pot downstairs. I brewed it for you."

"I don't suppose you'll bring me a cup."

"Sinead, I'll fetch you anything you'd like."

For a moment, just a moment, she believed him.

"None too worse for wear?"

"I'll never be able to use my arm again. It's probably pulled from the socket."

He put the mug on the nightstand and sat on the edge of the mattress. "I'll need your word that you won't run again."

"Quinn—"

"Your word, Sinead."

"This is intolerable." At this point, she'd do almost anything to be released from her bondage and for a cup of coffee.

She struggled to sit up, and he was there, silently helping her, lending his strength and his support. The sheets slipped, exposing her breasts and her hardening nipples.

The colour of his eyes seemed to darken.

As if he couldn't help himself, he leant forward.

Her back was against the headboard. Her arm was still tied. She had nowhere to go.

She knew his intent—it was telegraphed in the set of his jaw.

He cupped her left breast. Despite herself, her pussy moistened. *What is it about this man?* He squeezed her nipple between his thumb and forefinger.

"Perfect for clamps," he told her.

She shuddered.

He tightened his grip and her hips jerked.

He kept her breast cupped in his palm. He moved his head forward. After slowly releasing the taut nipple, he sucked the nub into his mouth. He gently bit, then he used his tongue to press the flesh against the back of his teeth.

"I could come from just this," she confessed.

He shook his head.

Denied the orgasm, she irrationally tried to scoot farther away, as if that would diminish the demanding need. But she was trapped, at his mercy.

He tightened the grip of his hand and plumped her flesh.

"I need you to stop, or I need permission to come."

He showed mercy.

With agonising deliberation, he released her, first the pressure on her nipple, then he moved his tongue completely away then he uncupped his hand.

It was then that she realised he'd showed no mercy.

She was totally hot for him. Her breaths were ragged. She curled the fingers of her free hand into a fist. The need for an orgasm throbbed an unrelenting demand.

He was a master, skilled at seduction. He knew *exactly* what he was doing.

"Where was I?" he asked. "Letting you go so you can come downstairs for a cup of coffee? Or tying your other arm and your legs and putting nipple clamps on you and watching your writhe as I use a lash lightly on your swollen cunt?"

Coffee was forgotten as that torturous image pushed her even closer to an orgasm. Her lips parted. "You really are a perfect sub. After coffee, I'll get out the clamps."

She nearly whimpered her disappointment.

"Before I release you, I'll have your word that you'll behave yourself in front of my grandmother."

"I don't know what kind of person you think I am," she snapped. "I will treat your grandmother with respect."

He nodded. He probably realised that was the best he could hope for.

It took him only a few seconds to unfasten her wrist. "Move slowly." He rubbed her wrist.

She gasped. A sharp pain shot through her arm. She hadn't been bound tightly. He'd left her plenty of slack so that she could move, but she was shocked by the pain of returning circulation.

He soothed her, stroking her hair. Then he completely distracted her by stroking her pussy.

She dug in her heels, arching towards him.

She'd rather have him an enemy than this. Kindness she didn't know what to do with.

"You're slick. In a word, perfect."

She didn't want to think of herself as his submissive. But her body objected to her mind's decision. Her body felt wanton. She craved his domination.

He continued to care for her until her arm felt nearly normal again.

This was a paradox she didn't know how to solve. He tied her, but he comforted her.

He helped her from the bed. "I'll give you five minutes in the toilet," he said. "Leave the door cracked open else I'll remove it from the hinges."

She pulled a sheet from the bed and wrapped it around her.

Sinead dashed for the bathroom. He brought his foot down, hard, on the sheet. The material floated to the floor. And damn him, the scowl she cast over her shoulder didn't seem to impress him at all.

In the bathroom, she collapsed against the wall.

Her emotions were topsy-turvy, her body ached. And thoughts of Jack Quinn crowded out everything else. They were sworn enemies, but more and more, she was having difficulty remembering that. How could a man so hated make her so weak?

Sinead took every moment of the allotted five minutes, and threw in an extra few seconds for good measure.

"Sinead?" He pushed the door open.

"Patience is not a virtue in your clan?"

"In the clan, aye. In me? No."

"And privacy?"

"Submissives receive none." He curved his hands around her upper arms and pulled her nude body close, then closer still. "For example, I want to fuck you thoroughly. Not just arouse you, mind you. I want to have my cock in you."

His arousal thrust against her belly. If it weren't for his trousers, she suspected he'd take her as he promised, as he threatened, despite the fact his grandmother awaited them.

He nipped at her right ear lobe.

"Quinn," she protested.

He laved the tiny hurt with the tip of his tongue.

Her nipples had remained hard. Her pussy still throbbed. He cupped a breast, as if weighing it. Juices flooded her.

146

At each turn, she proved him right. She was naturally submissive to him.

"Get dressed, lass, 'afore I change my mind."

"Maybe I'm hoping you changed your mind."

He laughed. The sound was as rich and intoxicating as the man himself.

"Your clothes are in the bottom two dresser drawers."

She pulled away from him and hurried to the corner of the room where he'd left her baggage. She was all-too-aware of him standing there, legs spread shoulder-width apart, arms folded as he watched her every move.

"If it 'twouldn't shock *máthair Chríona*, I'd keep you naked."

She donned a bra then pulled on a T-shirt.

"What fresh hell is this?" he asked, reading her the writing across her chest. He raised his brows.

She refused to be embarrassed. "It's not what I would usually select to meet someone's grandmother. Next time you kidnap me, buy me some clothes."

"The naked thing is sounding more tempting than ever."

A deadly, wicked gleam entered his blue eyes.

Quickly she wriggled into a skirt, just in case he was serious.

He held open the bedroom door and preceded her down the stairs, evidently not taking any chances.

She noticed that the front door was still bolted.

With an outstretched palm, he indicated she should precede him into the breakfast room.

The room was as striking as the rest of the home. Watercolours of outdoor scenes hung on the walls. There were several floor-to-ceiling windows with heavy drapes pulled back. Sunlight streamed in.

He announced their presence.

When the woman turned from one of the windows, he said, "*Mórai*, may I present Sinead O'Malley. Sinead, my grandmother, Catherine Quinn."

When he addressed his grandmother, his voice held a tender note. *Mórai* was an affectionate term, one he'd likely used since boyhood. It revealed another side she found dangerously appealing and endearing. The man was making it more and more difficult to hate him.

"Sinead. It's my pleasure." Tall and regal, Catherine Quinn resembled a warrior princess. Even though she leaned on a cane for support, the years had been kind. With grace and a simultaneous air of command, she crossed the room. She stopped in front of them and smiled brightly. The corners of the woman's eyes crinkled in genuine welcome.

Sinead was taken aback again.

She'd spent her life despising the Quinns and resenting their success and wealth. And yet the clan's matriarch seemed warm, holding no hostility.

Catherine leant on the cane with her left hand and extended her right hand, saying, "Thank you for accepting my invitation. I'm afraid I spent several sleepless nights afraid you wouldn't come."

Sinead fired a scowl at Jack. "I was given little choice in the matter, ma'am. It wasn't phrased as an invitation."

"Oh?" She shot her grandson a stern look. "Is that right, Jack?" Catherine asked.

He ran a finger beneath his collar.

Jack had warned her to mind her manners and she'd also been raised to respect her elders. But she couldn't fight her innate sense of fair play. She wanted his behaviour on the table. She didn't want Catherine believing she'd issued an invitation and that it had been cordially accepted. That would be dishonest.

She accepted Catherine's extended hand. "It seems your family has a history of kidnapping O'Malley women."

"Kidnapping, is it?" Catherine asked her grandson, her head cocked to the side.

"Sinead..." His soft word of warning was wrapped in a sheath of anger.

"He warned me to mind my manners with you," Sinead told Catherine. "I think I'm in for some terrible trouble now."

"Nonsense. My grandson is as kind as the day is long."

During winter in Siberia.

"Right," he agreed.

Catherine used her cane for support as she lowered herself into a high-backed chair at the head of the table. "Do not dare," she told Jack when he tried to assist her. "Men in this family," she said to Sinead. "Think they can solve everything for their women."

"Physically."

She heard his growl.

"Please have a seat, child," Catherine said, indicating the chair to her right. "And you," she told Jack, "can pour our guest a cup of tea, if you will." She indicated the sideboard, with a lovely teapot in a colourful cosy. An assortment of pastries was arranged on a two-tiered serving plate.

"Coffee, please," Sinead managed, as she took the seat. "The promise of a cup was the only thing that got me out of bed."

"Anything for your highness," he asked, clearly annoyed by her behaviour and his grandmother ordering him to fulfil host duties.

She smiled sunnily. "Of course. Perhaps a scone or croissant, as well. Chocolate something or other."

"The coffee is in the kitchen, I believe," Catherine told him.

"Yes, I know. I brewed it already."

Catherine cleared her throat. "Go on with you, my boy."

He clearly saw what his grandmother was about and he didn't like it. Well and all, wasn't that too bad? Sinead wanted a minute or two alone with the clan matriarch as much as Catherine seemed to want time with her.

"He's not a bad sort, actually," Catherine said after he left the room. She picked up her china cup, the nearly translucent porcelain appearing delicate in her grip.

"If you go for brutes."

The cup didn't even rattle as she returned it to its saucer. "He's a brute, is he?"

"Terrible."

"And you haven't blackened his eye?"

Sinead laughed. Suddenly she liked the older woman, especially as she hadn't raised a brow at Sinead's attire.

"He's terribly protective of me. And since the silver comb on my pillow..." She spread some butter on a cream cracker. "I'm afraid he's certain I'm going to pop off."

His tenderness towards his grandmother threatened, again, to melt Sinead's heart. She knew how irrational thoughts could be when love was involved. Hadn't she rung her mother incessantly until she dragged the woman from her bed? "The comb was on your pillow?"

"Aye, it was."

"But it shouldn't mean anything. The Banshee follows my family."

"There's more to the legend," Catherine said.

Jack re-joined them in a clatter of china and silver, interrupting the conversation.

Instead of sitting across from Sinead, at his grandmother's left hand, he took the chair next to Sinead.

He placed a mug of coffee in front of her then offered a plate containing a flaky croissant.

He moved his chair close to hers. Hoping to control her? Maybe use his presence to threaten her? Either way, he was in for a shock. Sinead wasn't easily intimidated. She tore off one end of the pastry. "Your grandmother wants to know why I haven't blackened your eye."

He choked on a drink of coffee.

"I've wondered the same thing. But since you've brought coffee, I'll tolerate you another few minutes." She took a sip. "Fabulous. Thank you. A bit more cream might have been nice."

"As you would say, wombat, bite me."

"Jack Neil Quinn," Catherine warned.

"Jack Neil Quinn," Sinead repeated. "That must be the name they call you when you're in trouble." Unaccountably she was enjoying her visit much more. "I'll bet you've been called by your full name rather frequently."

He dragged her chair ever closer to his. Uncomfortably close. Impolitely close.

Sinead inhaled the scent of him, that of Irish countryside and the hint of autumn rain.

He put his hand on her bare knee and squeezed.

It wasn't a polite touch, or even a warning grip. It was a promise of forthcoming retribution.

She didn't heed the warning, though, fool that she was.

As she took another sip of coffee, he tightened his grip.

She tried to stay still; she tried not to flinch. But damn it, in his grandmother's ancestral house, in the formal breakfast room, Sinead's pussy moistened.

She enjoyed goading Quinn. Part of her wanted to see how far she could push him. What in the name of creation was wrong with her? He intoxicated her. Since she'd had a taste of him, she wanted *more*. She wanted his punishment. She wanted him.

Boldly she closed her hand over his. Then she did something she'd never been brave enough to do before. She guided his hand up her thigh towards her moist core.

Unerringly, he fingered her clit.

She jerked, already *that close*. Dear God. Now that she'd started it, she realised he'd finish it.

She reached for her coffee, clattering the fine china. "I'd love another cup," she managed, praying she could hold back a gasp.

He smiled. He pinched her clit.

She gritted her teeth.

"I'll have a refresh on my tea as well, my boy."

He flipped Sinead's skirt back into position then scooted his chair back from the table.

"You were telling me about the Banshee," Sinead managed, struggling to focus on something other than her body's insistent demands.

Catherine laced her hands on top of the table. "According to lore, you're correct, the Banshee traditionally only follows certain families. But since Agnes's curse, the Banshee also heralds death for the Quinns. That explains why the comb I found on my pillow has your family crest."

"I'm confused," Sinead admitted. And she was sure it had nothing to do with Jack's proximity.

"You know the story of the Quinns and O'Malleys," Catherine said.

"'Tis chronicled in the *Annals of the Four Masters*. And of course she knew her family's side of the tale.

"The facts, aye," Catherine agreed, "but not the details. Not the reasons."

"Go on," Sinead encouraged. "Please." She wanted to hear the Quinn side of the tale.

"Our family raided your keep."

This much, Sinead knew.

Catherine shuddered. "So much bloodshed, on both sides. So much anger, and could have been avoided."

Jack reached across Sinead to top off his grandmother's tea. Intentionally, Sinead was sure, he crowded her.

After Catherine added a healthy splash of milk to her cup and stirred it a dozen times more than needed, she continued, "Your family kept sheep, you know. And the Quinns were hungry. One of their children was near to starving, if the legend is true."

"I beg your pardon?"

"Aye. The child's mother went right to the hold and begged for food."

"And she was turned away?"

"She was afraid for her child, desperate for herself and her clansmen, I suppose. She tried to steal a lamb, but the O'Malleys forcibly took it back. Angered by the way she was treated, my Quinn ancestors led an attack on your keep. Unforgivable. Yet I understand no physical harm was intended. They decided to take all the sheep."

Sinead slumped in her chair. She'd never heard this side of the story. Did not make it untrue, however.

"During the raid, your ancestor, the lovely Bridget, caught the eye of my relation. She was standing atop a hill, as legend has it. It was foggy, but her fiery red hair seemed to be alight. She was indignant, protecting her family. Even though she was a woman, she took up a sword to join the battle."

A woman after Sinead's own heart.

"The Quinns disarmed her, but they found they couldna hurt her. So they took her and refused to let her go."

"They kidnapped her. Some things never change," Sinead said. She levelled a look at Jack

"Right, then."

Despite his grandmother being there, he shoved back his chair and. With deadly efficiency he yanked her from her seat, toppling the chair. He dragged her against him and claimed her mouth forcefully.

He thrust his tongue into her mouth, demanding her submission; demanding contrition.

She told herself she didn't want him or his domination. She didn't want this. Didn't.

Did.

Damn it.

He kept at it until she responded with the passion he wanted, mindless, it seemed, that his grandmother was sipping her tea.

"Now," he said, ending the kiss, "unless you want me to turn you over my knee, here and now and blister your behind, you'll mind your manners."

She gasped. "You wouldn't."

"Try me." His hands on her shoulders were tight, relentless, but not painful. "There's a reason my relations kidnap yours. To shut you up."

"I…" She started to protest, then thought better of it and shut her mouth.

"Better," he approved. "Much better."

Catherine regarded the two over the rim of her cup. Rather than chastising her ill-mannered grandson, she smiled.

Jack righted Sinead's chair.

Sinead collapsed breathlessly back into it.

"Now then, where was I?" Catherine returned her cup and saucer to the table.

Sinead's hand shook as she reached for her own cup. The man unnerved her. His grandmother seemed not to mind at all that her grandson was manhandling their *guest*. Sinead wanted to escape, but another, naughty part of her wanted to surrender completely. She'd never been more confused, more challenged, more aroused.

"Be a dear and refill my cup," Catherine told Jack as if they were all watching a polite game of croquet. Then she continued. "As I was saying, our relation Cormac Quinn fell in love with Bridget. Instead of holding her for ransom like the family demanded, he decided to run away with her. Cormac's father was furious with his youngest son and went after the pair. The elder Quinn took up his sword against Cormac."

Jack topped up his grandmother's tea. Catherine used the pause for dramatic effect before saying, "Bridget stepped in front of the sword."

"She was killed?" Sinead asked.

"Aye. That she was. Cormac returned his beloved's body to her family. Devastated by the loss of her youngest child, Bridget's mother swore a curse on the Quinns, tying the fates of the two clans together."

Sinead might not believe in curses, but the story was fascinating.

"Bridget's mother wanted the Quinns to feel the same pain as she did. She wanted them to experience the same loss, the same devastation. There have been no spectacular relationships in our lineage for hundreds of years."

Jack picked up the thread. "Death, desertion, not marrying at all has plagued us. Because of Irish law, divorce has not been an option until recently, although I'm sure relations of mine have wished for the opportunity."

"That happens in every family," Sinead said.

Catherine nodded. "But there has rarely been more than one child born of any Quinn union. You'll have to admit that's unusual."

Sinead nodded at that. "For the most part," she conceded. "But the same is true of my family."

"Indeed, we're tied together, thanks to Bridget's mother, Agnes. The few marriages that seemed blessed and lasted were virtually child-free. Too many marriages have been cut short by accidents, by war, by untimely death, far too many than can be rationally explained."

Sinead believed there was a rational explanation for everything, or rather she had believed in rational explanations until Jack showed up and she found a silver comb in her Denver hotel room.

"According to legend, Agnes was a witch. When she swore out the curse, bones rattled in their graves, the sun went behind the clouds, darkness fell."

"Probably an eclipse," Jack said.

She couldn't agree more.

Catherine scowled before continuing, "Agnes proclaimed that the curse could only be lifted by an O'Malley once again choosing a Quinn," Catherine continued.

"We can leave this for future generations, then," Sinead said. "Because I certainly am not choosing a Quinn." She'd rather continue her tour, pouring her energies into replenishing the family coffers, and forgetting the orgasms Jack Quinn had given her. Surely there was another man out there who could give her what she wanted?

"You could make that choice and no one would blame you. Until I found the silver comb, I would have agreed with you. But I'm an old woman, Sinead. I too grew up despising your relatives. But I no longer see the point in continuing this nonsense. Until the curse is lifted, our families are joined together. Births, deaths, failed marriages. You two have a chance to end it once and for all, freeing your children."

I'm sorry. I can't help. I have no desire to marry. And if I did, I wouldn't choose Jack."

"Because he's a brute?" Catherine asked.

Sinead sighed.

"You're descended from the mighty Bridget," Catherine told her. "What would you have from a man who is your equal? A simpleton, perhaps? Or mayhap a doormat? Or do you prefer a man who will accept you and your strengths? A man who will challenge you as much as you challenge him?"

Sinead thought back to Donal and to the other failed relationships in her life. None of them had given her a challenge. None had inflamed her blood. "I understand that you would want this," she said. "Truly I do. But I want nothing to do with the Quinns. I've accepted your invitation. I've heard your story. And my answer is no. If you'll excuse me…"

"Sinead…"

"I won't run." When she saw his brows draw together, she added, "I'll let you or one of your people drive me home. It was a pleasure, ma'am," she told Catherine. "I wish you health."

He stood while she left the table.

He was such a contradiction. A masterful Dominant, an ill-mannered lout, and a solicitous lover.

"I'll be up in ten minutes. Be prepared."

Desire scorched her cheeks.

She shouldn't want him. She should remain firm in her decision to leave. But, damn, this man made her respond in ways she never had before.

Chapter Eight

"Give her time," Catherine advised.

"Keep her tied up is more like it." He scowled. "She needs a good hiding and to be locked in a dungeon somewhere."

"As I asked Sinead, what would you have, *Garmhac*?" she asked, calling him 'grandson of the heart'. "There's a reason you've not married."

He remembered the loss, the anguish. He'd given his heart to her, imagined a future together. "Maeve's betrayal."

"Posh. More likely you haven't found a woman who challenged you," Catherine observed with surprising insight.

He could always count on his grandmother to tell the truth.

"No doubt you're wary, as you have a right to be. But you've not got a hardened heart. You've had a host of women since Maeve. And honestly, my darling child, I think you and Maeve would have divorced afore now. You were smitten. But she ultimately wouldn't have been what you wanted."

He winced, not because she was brutal in her directness, but because she was probably right.

His grandmother was correct on another point as well. The O'Malley woman fascinated him. She tied him up just as surely as he'd bound her the night before. Her responses were passionate and uninhibited. He couldn't think of much beyond shoving his cock inside her while she screamed his name. "If you'll excuse me?" he said to his grandmother.

She placed her hand on his. "It could be that you'll love this one, Jack. Take her away. See what happens."

Banshees, curses and love were for others less fanciful than he. But all that aside, what harm would there be in joining the clans? From a pragmatic approach, his grandmother's argument was solid enough. Their lands adjoined each other. Both families would benefit from joint ownership. And if there were no more bad blood, that was simply a bonus.

"Go to her," Catherine told him. "Do not let her get away."

He excused himself and headed upstairs.

He heard the water running in the shower, which meant she'd followed his order to be naked.

He moved towards the bathroom, realising she'd also left the door open.

His cock hardened. Having this woman obey him so completely affected him in a way he'd never experienced before.

He braced his shoulder against the doorjamb. Shamelessly he watched her. Even though the glass was wavy, she was a picture of loveliness.

She poured shampoo into her palm then lathered her hair.

Her movements were graceful and erotic in their innocence.

He could think of nothing but bending her over the bed, tying her hands behind her back and taking her from behind.

After she rinsed her hair, she looked over at him.

To her credit, she didn't change what she was doing. She soaped her body then used the handheld showerhead to rinse.

Steam billowed over the top of the door and fogged the edges of the mirror. It gave the small room an even greater air of intimacy.

"Shave your pussy," he told her. "I want you smooth and bare. Always."

He watched, aroused, as she did.

When she turned off the water, he grabbed a towel from the rack. She slid open the glass door and stepped onto a mat.

"Allow me," he offered.

She moistened her lower lip but stood still.

His grandmother was right about one thing. He did want a woman who challenged him. And one who alternately challenged and surrendered was irresistible.

He towel-dried her hair then gently wiped her face and neck.

"Jack…"

"Sir," he corrected her. "Or Master, if you prefer."

"I don't."

"I do. And I'll have you calling me Master as you come."

She didn't answer. Maybe she was smart enough not to argue.

He moved the towel across her chest.

Her nipples pebbled, whether from his touch or from the chill of cooling water, he had no idea.

He wiped the moisture from her breasts. Then he moved lower, across her ribs, the alluring swell of her belly. "Spread your legs." She followed his orders. He dried her bare cunt, then the inside of her toned thighs. He knelt in front of her to dry her lower legs. And since he was there, he placed a kiss on her pubis.

"Jack…"

"Tell me what you want. Be specific. Be graphic."

"I want…"

"Tell me."

"Lick my pussy."

"How?"

She dug her hands into his hair. "What do you mean?"

"Lick me gently, Sir. Lick me hard, please, Sir," he coached. "Lick me gently until I start to come then bite my swollen clit. Or maybe slap my cunt as hard as you can then suck my clit until I scream."

" —lick," she said.

"Tell me within three seconds, wench, or you can get dressed."

He saw the rapid rise and fall of her ribcage.

"No embarrassment," he reminded her.

She looked down at him. He held her gaze captive.

The woman might refuse to marry him, might say she didn't want anything to do with him, but her body betrayed her. As for him, he was simply a man, a Dom. No matter what existed between them, he couldn't not give her what she craved, what they both craved.

"I shouldn't…"

On his knees, one palm pressed to the small of her back, he waited, allowing the seconds to pass. He wouldn't force her, but he knew she wanted this as much as he did.

She swallowed hard before saying, "Lick me gently, then slap my cunt, then suck my clit until I come."

His cock tightened. His pulse thundered in his ears. Having her be so responsive thrilled him. "Sir," he added.

"Sir," she repeated.

His cock demanded immediate release. Her voice, low and sultry, inflamed his ardour.

He swept her from the floor and carried her into the next room where he placed her on the edge of the bed. "Stay where you are and lie back. Keep your legs apart." When he had her positioned as he wanted, knees spread, he told her, "Place your hands beneath the small of your back. If you can't control yourself, if you try to shield your pussy from my slaps, you'll be tied. Unless you want to be tied?"

She shook her head.

"I beg your pardon?"

"Please leave my arms loose, Sir."

He knelt before her and placed his hands on her inner thighs to keep her legs apart. Then he gently tongued the length of her pussy. He carefully watched her reactions to know where, exactly, he elicited the sweetest response.

He gently laved her clit and noticed that she thrashed her head back and forth. He grinned.

He increased the pressure and the tempo then pulled back to spank her cunt.

Shockingly, she screamed out an orgasm.

He'd been prepared to play with her, torment her for long minutes, but the perfect little sub had shattered in only seconds, and from a simple slap. He waited.

"Thank you, Sir," she managed.

He considered giving her more. But he liked her a little needy. "Your pussy is beautifully red and swollen," he said. "Put on a skirt and your T-shirt and a pair of shoes and socks. Nothing more."

She struggled into a sitting position.

"You've been kidnapped," he reminded her. "If you think I'm letting you go that easily, you're wrong."

"You're going to forcefully keep me here?" she demanded.

Her eyes were a curious mixture of heat and anger. And if he didn't keep control of himself, he'd sink his dick in her to the hilt. "I'm going to try and convince you to willingly marry me."

"Really? What's to stop you grabbing me by the hair and dragging me down the aisle?"

He stood. "Nothing at all. We have a family chapel and a priest. Would you like me to do that?"

"*Gobshite.*"

"I'll take that insult as a rejection of my proposal."

She wrapped her arms around her middle.

"We'll be leaving in my car," he informed her. "Liam packed your bag while we had breakfast. Now, it's your choice of how you get in my car. Fully dressed and willing. Or I can carry you naked. While he was here, Liam left us a gag if you choose the second option." He crossed the room, took her case from the wardrobe, and picked up the gag that Liam had left with it.

"You—"

"Would," he countered, making a show of pocketing the gag. "With my grandmother's blessing."

In the end, unfortunately, she chose to wear clothes and walk to the car of her own free will while he dealt with their cases.

His grandmother saw them off as if they were going on holiday.

"This is under duress," Sinead said.

"Blacken his eye, then."

He drove to the shore and met up with Logan, a manservant and boat pilot. Jack had rung Logan earlier and arranged for the man to ferry them across Clew Bay.

The weather was nippy, as he expected, and Logan pulled out a blanket. Jack wrapped it around her shoulders. "You could have let me put on a jacket."

"Then your nipples wouldn't have been so hard."

"Male logic?"

"What other kind is there?"

"Your woman is beautiful," Logan told Jack.

"Aye. She is."

He offered her a glass of wine that she turned down. Fine with him. He preferred to play with totally sober subs.

When they landed, he helped her ashore, not at all disappointed when the wind licked at the hem of her skirt and made it ride just a little higher.

"Where are we?" she asked.

"Your temporary home."

"Is the island inhabited?"

He shook his head.

Sinead wrapped her arms around her middle to ward off the afternoon chill. Wind whipped through the trees and spat sea water at them.

He took off his jacket and helped her into it, surprisingly, ridiculously delighted in how big it was on her. "It will be just us here. Peace. Quiet. Solitude. And your fantasies coming true. Including the ones with Logan."

Her eyes widened. He did love shocking her.

"With Logan?"

"Indeed. You'll have a choice in the matter."

She was silent.

"As to which of us you want up your arse and which you want stuffing your cunt."

She shivered. But she licked her lower lip and glanced at the ground. She was shocked. But she hadn't protested.

His grandmother's words returned. What did he want from a woman, indeed? And there was something to the fact he hadn't chosen another after Maeve. Truth was, as much as he'd loved her they hadn't been entirely suited. Sex had been good, but kink hadn't been her thing. After that, he'd decided not to be with a woman who wasn't his match mentally, physically or sexually.

Against her ear he added, "Before that, if you've a mind, I can bend you over a tree branch and use my belt on your exposed arse. Or I can tie you to a tree while I eat your pussy. I can even use a tree branch to secure your hands above your head while I whip you for your earlier impertinence. You can scream as long as you like, as loud as you like, and the only thing you'll disturb will be the birds. And Logan will definitely enjoy the sight."

She gasped. "You wouldn't."

"Aye. I would. And I'd even let Logan have a turn while you sucked my cock. Don't think I've forgotten I owe you a punishment for your behaviour at breakfast."

Sinead stood there, mouth open a bit like a fish out of water while Logan gathered their luggage.

She rounded on Jack. "Logan knows?"

"That you're my intended? That you're my sub? That you'll be punished for your behaviour? Yes, all of it. We routinely share subs. I told you about him, without mentioning his name."

"You're—"

"Ready to get on with it. And unless you're wanting to strip right here and right now and take your punishment, I suggest you get your beautiful rear into the cottage."

She scowled, then, obviously choosing her battles, she tipped back her chin—after all, she didn't come from a line of warriors for nothing—and preceded him to the house.

The door was unlocked, and the insides were fairly inviting. He'd sent Logan ahead to prepare the place, including the playroom.

Huge rugs adorned the floors. A hearth was the focal point of the living room, and soaring windows let in the sunlight, such as it was. A settee and wing-backed chair were set at angles near the already-blazing fireplace. Leather-bound books adorned the wooden shelving. It wasn't luxury, but it was comfortable enough and a place for him to be alone...or not, as the case might be.

"The place suits you."

She was right. The island was beautiful in a rugged way that appealed to him. Lush, verdant, with soaring trees and wildflowers blooming in dazzling splashes of colour.

They were near enough to see the mainland and the soaring mountain that was Croagh Patrick, the most famous in all of Ireland, most of Europe for that matter. 'Twas the place of legend and pilgrimage where thousands climbed each year, barefoot, in memory of Saint

Patrick himself, who fasted for forty days and nights at the craggy, hostile summit some fifteen hundred years before.

"We even have running water. Civilisation by any standards." He'd give up all his worldly goods before he'd give up this slice of heaven. "Provisions have already been delivered so you don't have to forage for food."

"Me?"

"I'm lord and master of all I survey. You're the servant."

"We all live to serve you, Sir," Logan said, walking past them to carry their bags into the master bedroom.

She looked at Logan's retreating figure, then back at him, as if trying to decide whether or not Logan was serious.

"Tell me your safe word."

"*Dearg.*"

"Just that?" He wanted to be very clear that she knew her safe word, that if she felt out of control, she could stop. "Or will *red* serve as a substitute?"

She shook her head. "*Dearg,*" she said.

"You have your safety net," he told her. "Really you have the control. But you also have the freedom to experience your wildest desires. If you shout no, I will not stop. That, too, gives you freedom. Do you understand?"

She nodded.

"Tell me."

"I know…" She paused to swallow.

"Look me in the eye. I want to be sure we're clear."

Obediently, wonderfully, she met his gaze. "I can stop the scene by using my safe word. The word no will not stop the scene."

"Remove your clothes."

She blinked. "But Logan—"

"Remove your clothes, Sinead, unless you'd like me to strip them off you?" He folded his arms implacably across his chest. "I told you to expect this. I told you we could talk about it after you've tried it, but not before. Logan is a loyal manservant. And I'm inviting him into the scene."

"I've never done anything like this."

"There's a lot you've never done," he countered. He watched the internal struggle that waged on her face, from the way she drew her lower lip between her teeth to the way she glanced towards the bedroom, to the way a small frown furrowed her brow. Watching her closely was akin to reading her mind. "You want this," he guessed, "and you wish you didn't. You're curious. Part of you hopes I'll simply push so that you're absolved of responsibility. And you wish the one Dom who intends to have you were anyone but the man you see as a mortal enemy."

"You could have a job at a carnival." She paused. "As a soothsayer."

She ventured a grin that he didn't return.

The fireplace snapped and crackled. "Will there be any...repercussions if you undress me?"

"None. That question came without a penalty. But clever of you to ask."

She looked down at the ground.

"Better yet," he said. "Logan can strip you."

When she didn't protest, he called out Logan's name.

The other man entered the living room. "Sir?"

"Kindly undress my sub while I watch. Sinead, remove your shoes and socks."

After she'd followed orders, stuffing her socks inside her shoes then scooting them beneath the settee, she returned to a standing position. Logan moved behind her so he didn't obstruct Jack's view.

The other man grabbed the bottom of Sinead's T-shirt and pulled it up over her head.

She looked so appealing standing there, her upper body bare, but still dressed in her skirt. Her nipples were already taut. His trousers were already tight. "Sinead enjoys nipple stimulation."

"Indeed, Sir." The man cradled her full breasts in his palms. Then, while Jack watched, the man gently pinched her nipples. "Look at me, Sinead." He wanted to gauge her reaction, to see when pleasure became pain and pain became pleasure.

She met his gaze.

"A bit more pressure," he told Logan.

Wordlessly the man followed the command.

Her eyes widened.

"More," Jack said.

"Sir," she protested.

"More," Jack repeated.

Her nostrils flared. "Good," he said quietly. "Lovely. Now just a bit more, Logan. Pull her nipples up and away from her breasts."

She yelped.

"School yourself," he told her.

She squeezed her eyes closed. She was still feeling pain and fighting it. He wanted her to move past it. "Now twist her nipples," he instructed.

With deliberate motions, Logan did as he was told.

"Sir!" she shouted.

"Breathe, Sinead. You can take it. Logan, give her more. Harder." He crossed the distance separating them and thrust his hand beneath her skirt, unerringly finding her pussy. "You're drenched," he observed. "More pressure on her nipples." He stroked her wet folds. She rocked her hips back and forth, seeking to get off.

The tension between her brows eased. "You're liking it more now?" he asked. "More pleasure than pain?"

"I want to come."

"Release her," he instructed Logan.

"Sir!"

He pulled his hand away simultaneously, leaving her on the edge. Her shoulders slumped forward. "Good girl."

"Good girl? I want to use a curse word."

"You may not." He kept the grin off his face. "Logan, her skirt, if you will."

The man lowered the zip and pulled the material down, past her hips and dropped it to the wooden floor.

"Step out of the skirt," he told her, "then kneel up."

She moved slowly as if trying to compute his order.

She knelt. As he'd taught her, she spread her knees apart, placed her hands behind her neck and arched slightly so her chest stuck out. She cast her gaze towards the floor. "Perfect," he said. "Now for the next position. Pay attention and repeat it back to me."

She nodded.

"It's called present." He noticed her twitch a bit. She wasn't terribly experienced, but she was fairly well read. Obviously she had some idea of what to expect. "On your back. Raise your knees, allow your legs to fall to the sides, cup your knees in your palms for support. The purpose is for me to be able to look at your pussy. I'll be able to see if you're properly groomed. If I requested you insert a plug, I'll be able to see if you did that. I'll be able to see if you are wet. And I'll be able to show you to anyone I please. Explain the position to me."

"Uhm…"

"No prevarication," he snapped.

"I lie on my back, Sir, with my legs spread, my knees raised and supported by my hands."

"You will maintain your position as you're inspected."

She nodded.

"Present."

With grace unexpected in one so untrained, she assumed the position. Obviously her dance training enhanced the experience.

When she was completely exposed, he crouched between her legs. "When I tell you to shave, I expect the insides of your pussy lips to feel just like this..." He smoothed his thumbs on the inside of her labia. "Smooth and bare. Understand?"

"Yes, Sir."

"I do like your pussy wet." He finger-fucked her hard.

"Yes, Sir!"

"And I like to see your arsehole stretched in anticipation of my penetration." He traced a damp finger around that puckered place. "I will do all of these things when I inspect you. Logan, inspect my submissive. Sinead, behave yourself."

He stood.

Logan, always the perfect submissive and manservant, offered him a towel. When he had Sinead anticipating his needs and desires like this... Aye. There was a fantasy. He'd sooner meet the Banshee on the beach than he'd have Sinead trained.

Logan knelt between her legs.

He inspected her a bit differently than Jack had, which was good. Let her not always know what to anticipate.

Logan smoothed one of his big callused hands down her intimate area, from pubic bone to anus. He used his left hand to spread her pussy lips. With his right forefinger, he felt the inside of each fold. "Smooth here, as well."

Moving quickly, he inserted two fingers in her damp pussy.

Through his pants, Jack stroked his cock. He'd watched Logan with his women before, but he'd never been this aroused.

"Vagina is nice and moist," Logan commented. "Sir, do you have any lubricant?"

He saw Sinead swallow deeply. She closed her eyes, but she didn't protest. "Indeed." He went into the playroom and fetched a pump bottle of lube and placed it within easy reach.

He crossed his arms. If he wasn't mistaken, his manservant's breathing had become more laboured. No wonder. She was a total delight. "Keep your legs apart," he told Sinead. "When I give someone else permission to inspect you or play with you, you follow that person's orders as if he were me. He's your master as surely as I am."

He knew she was still nervous to have someone near her most private hole, but the sooner she got past it, the better.

He trusted Logan with her. But he also knew the man was a little more aggressive than he was.

Logan pumped a dollop of lube onto his forefinger. He entered her quickly.

She gasped at the intrusion and released her grip on her knees.

"Position," he told her.

Logan gave her no recovery time, moving his finger about, side to side, up and down, stretching her wider.

"Position," Jack snapped.

Logan was relentless, but she was amazing, getting hold of her knees and remaining still. "Glad we don't have to make your upcoming punishment worse," he told her.

Logan continued to move his finger inside her. Even from the distance, Jack noticed her pussy glistening with moisture. She would enjoy the double penetration, he knew it. "Kneel up."

Logan moved away from her. She blinked several times, staring at the ceiling. "You do not want me to repeat my order."

As if coming back into her body, she moved quickly and gracefully.

"Logan, fetch a pair of clover clamps from the playroom."

"Certainly, Sir."

As his manservant went to the play room, Jack informed her, "I'm going to clamp your nipples."

"Yes, Sir."

"And you will thank me. We'll move to the spanking bench in the playroom, and you'll crawl there. When you're positioned, you'll ask Logan to place a plug in your arse. You'll be tied, and you'll feel my lash. You'll receive several extra lashes for your lack of gratitude for your gentle inspection."

She gulped in several drinks of air.

"It could have been much worse," he told her. "For example... Present!"

She got into position, and he crouched in the same place he had earlier. Instead of a gentle touch, he used a lot of pressure against her skin as he felt her external pubis for hair.

"I understand, Sir!"

He pinched her right labia between his right thumb and forefinger then pulled back the flesh and harshly felt the inside flesh.

"Sir! Please!"

"You'll learn gratitude, Miss." He repeated the procedure on her left labia.

"Thank you, Sir." Her face contorted with pain.

He abruptly let her go. Her skin was reddened from the handling, and she'd never looked more beautiful to him. He pulled back the tiny hood of her clitoris and pinched the tender flesh before instantly releasing her. She thrashed from side to side and he shoved two fingers inside her moist core and forced another in her arse.

"Oh my God, Sir!"

He lifted her body from the ground with that brutal grip.

"Sir! Thank you! Thank you for the inspection, Sir!"

"You'll be wanting to thank Logan for being so gentle, as well."

"Yes, Sir. Thank you."

"Lesson over." He gentled his tone. "I hope it was well learned."

She was all but panting when he released her. And the submissive little vixen was completely wet. He hadn't been gentle, but she hadn't safe worded out.

"Thank you," she said again and again.

Logan had returned to the room. He held out the clamps. "She's a responsive one, Sir."

"Thank you, Logan," she told the man. "For being so gentle with your inspection."

"Oh, the Master would have my cock baked in a lasagne if I wasn't."

"Kneel up."

She instantly transitioned into position.

"I believe I'd like you to stand," he amended.

She did.

"Arms behind your neck, as if you were kneeling. Legs apart, toes turned slightly outward."

As he spoke, she did as he asked.

"Logan, come up behind her. That's a lad. Cup her right breast and squeeze her nipple, get it nice and hard for the clamp."

When their gazes met, she lowered hers. "Quick study." After this, how could she deny she was meant to be his?

When Logan released her nipple, Jack clamped it.

"Ow! Ow, ow, ow, ow, ow!"

"That doesn't sound like thank you," Jack mentioned.

"Thank you, ow, Sir!"

"Breathe, *muirnín*."

While she struggled go get herself under control, he and Logan repeated the process on her other nipple. Within seconds, the silver chain draped between her breasts.

"That will intensify all the other things you're experiencing," he told her after she'd expressed her gratitude. "Now, get down on all fours. Crawl into the playroom."

Her chin was set in a mutinous tilt. He waited, wondering. Then she did as he'd told her.

At this point, it didn't much matter to him what she thought about marriage. She was going to be his. She could struggle and fight all she wanted. But the lass would be his forever. The curse would be a convenient excuse. But their combined pleasure was the real reason. His grandmother's happiness would be a double bonus.

He followed her, watching the feminine sway of her hips and enjoying the sight of the metal chain that dipped towards the floor.

"I want her on the edge of the bench," he told Logan. "I want her arse plump for the whipping. Allow her knee supports, but secure her wrists at the bottom so she can't pull up."

The bench had been built by Logan himself. It had a long padded board that ran across the top. The side supports had plenty of different places to insert knee supports, if wanted. And there were numerous hooks to secure a sub's hands or feet. The bench was customisable for each person. He could secure a man such as Logan as easily as a bonny lass such as Sinead.

"Can we take off the clamps?" she asked.

"Absolutely not. Ask again and your punishment will be worse."

Logan glanced at her then at the bench. "Lie length-wise across the top."

She shot Jack a desperate glance. "Get on with it." Indeed, he couldn't wait to fuck her while her arse was reddened from his flogger.

Logan placed her knees in the supports then checked his work by moving her back a bit so her arse was completely jutting towards Jack. Jack wasn't sure he would survive the beating.

Logan used lengths of fabric to secure her thighs and severely restrict her motions.

While Jack selected a flogger, Logan fastened her wrists near the floor.

Jack crouched next to her. "You're going to thank Logan for his excellent work then you'll ask him to put that little plug up your arse." He put a hand in her hair. "You may think to be grateful that he took the time to stretch your hole while he inspected you. It'll make the penetration easier."

She nodded.

"This is a flogger." He held the implement in his hand. "It has a dozen thick leather thongs. It's for beginners. It's thicker, more thuddy than others we'll use in the future. When we're doing a pleasure beating, you may opt for this."

"Pleasure beating?"

"I promise, it exists. But not until you're significantly better behaved. Make no mistake, you'll still feel the effects of this one. Since this is only your second punishment, I will still go easy. In future, I'll expect that you'll ask me to hit you harder and harder."

Her eyes widened.

"You'll see."

She shook her head.

"How are you doing?"

"Nervous. Scared. Anxious."

"Safe word?"

"I don't want to use it."

"Damn," he said. "You impress me at turns, Sinead."

"I want this."

"Any exposed part of your body is subject to my lash," he cautioned her.

"I understand."

He smoothed his knuckles down the curve of her cheekbone before standing. "It's up to you," he told her. "You may address Logan as Sir."

"Isn't he a submissive?" she asked.

"My submissive," Jack agreed. "But superior to you."

"Please, Sir Logan, put a plug up my arse. And thank you for securing me well."

Logan fetched another bottle of lube. He lubricated his first two fingers. He inserted them, one at a time, inside her, giving her time to accommodate him, making her hole bigger for the insertion.

"That'll be enough," Jack said when she was moving her hips in time to Logan's thrusting fingers. She was hopeless. Apparently she'd got a taste of illicitness and craved more. Suddenly he was afraid he wouldn't be able to keep up.

Logan put the plug in place, and she didn't moan half as much as Jack had expected.

"Well done," Logan told her.

"I think you rather enjoyed doing that to our little sub."

"Aye, Sir. I did."

"For your troubles, you can fetch a cock ring."

Logan's eyes darkened with desire and a bit of frustration. "A cock ring, Sir?"

"Now, Logan. Now."

Logan remained immobilised for a few seconds. But without further question, he moved towards the cabinet and returned with a small rubber cock ring.

"Took you a little long to respond," Jack said as he placed the flogger across Sinead's shoulders and extended his palm to accept the rubber ring from his other sub.

"Aye, Sir. Unforgivable."

There was nothing more arousing to Jack than this scene. Two perfect subs, willing to try anything. "How long since you've felt my belt?"

"A very long time, Sir. Too long."

He needed this. His man needed this. And he wanted Sinead to see an experienced sub take a punishment. It hadn't been planned, but there it was. "Are you hard or flaccid, sub?"

"Hard, Sir."

"We'll take care of that. Remove everything from the waist down."

He noticed Sinead staring.

His manservant hurriedly stripped.

"Your erection is impressive."

"Aye, Sir."

Reaching out, he squeezed Logan's gorgeous cock in precisely the right spot and with the perfect amount of pressure to diminish the hardness.

Logan released a breath through his closed teeth before saying, "Thank you for dispensing with my undesired erection, Sir."

"You haven't masturbated without permission?"

"It's been a long time since I came last, Sir."

"Answer the question," he snapped, even though he knew the answer. It had, indeed, been a long time since he beat his man so hard he spurted on the bench.

"No, Master. I am not permitted to masturbate, and remaining true to Master's demands is important in proper submission."

"Well said." When the man was sufficiently softened, Jack rolled the cock ring down to the base of the shaft. "Good thing you're clean-shaven."

"Aye, Sir. Always in anticipation of your arrival."

He glanced over at Sinead. "I expect the same from you."

She nodded mutely.

He squeezed his man's balls, manipulating them as he placed the ring even farther down.

"Thank you, Sir. That ought to keep your sub's erection under control."

"If not, it will be terribly uncomfortable."

"If it pleases, Master."

"It does." He was completely aware of Sinead's mixture of shock and awe. She'd remained strangely silent, though. "I'm going to blister your arse."

"Yes, Master. Thank you, Master."

The man's voice had taken on a hazy, distant quality. He hoped to one day hear something similar from Sinead. "We clamped Sinead's nipples."

"She has gorgeous tits, Master. Master should consider clamping her breasts as well as her nipples."

"I'll consider it. For now, I think it's only fair we weight your balls."

"If it pleases, Master."

Jack crossed the room and selected a couple of weights. The idea of seeing his man's testicles dangling, pulled even lower for Jack's pleasure was nearly more than he could take.

If he didn't get on with it, he'd need to masturbate in another room. Two gorgeous subs, both awaiting his pleasure... He'd need less than a dozen strokes to shoot his load. What kind of restraint was that?

He affixed the weights, loving the way each of Logan's pebbles felt in their sack. The man sucked in a steadying breath before expressing his gratitude. "May the sub suck Master's cock to show his appreciation?"

"You can take your punishment. Reach for the floor." Jack focused his attention on his motions as he removed his belt, knowing if he didn't, he'd fumble like a first-time Dom. He wanted Sinead to see nothing but confidence. "How many? Be specific."

"Eight, if it pleases Master."

"Eight it is." He pulled the belt free of the last loop. He doubled it over. "Do you see, Sinead, how he answers direct questions?"

"Yes," she whispered.

He took a step back to admire Logan and his tight buttocks. He noticed Sinead watching.

The weights swung, pulling down Logan's balls.

"That has to hurt," Sinead said, shifting on the bench.

"Is it painful, sub?" he asked, tugging on the metal weights.

"Indeed, Sir. It is. But I find pleasure in Master's pleasure. If it pleases Sir to subject his lowly sub to pain, then your sub is pleased."

He knew the man meant it.

Logan hadn't broken position, despite the obvious pain, and his hands were firmly wrapped around his ankles.

Jack steadied himself. He never approached a sub without being in total control. "You may avert your gaze," he said to Sinead. "Or you may watch."

"I…"

He laid the leather blisteringly across his man's buttocks.

He sighed. "Thank you, Sir."

There was such a difference between Sinead's begrudging words of thanks and his man's heartfelt gratitude.

Jack placed the next searingly in the same spot.

"Sir is so masterful. Thank you."

He looked at Sinead. Her eyes were wide and unblinking. She seemed somewhat transfixed, and not at all in a bad way.

He moved the next lower then lower still. On the seventh, he caught Logan below his buttocks.

"Sir! Thank you! Jesus, Mary and Joseph, Sir, you make me want to come, cock ring or no."

"Mayhap this will help." He tempered the next one. And he knew Logan knew what to expect. With the tip of his belt, he caught Logan's testicles. Logan's knees buckled, but Jack saw his cock straining against its confining ring.

"Thank you, Sir." The man choked on a sob.

"Spread your legs wider."

Unquestioningly he did as instructed.

Jack was aware of Sinead following his every move as he placed his belt on a hook protruding from the wall. He washed his hands in the small sink before lubing his forefinger and returning to slowly sink deep in Logan's arse in order to manipulate the man's prostate.

"I need to come, Master."

"Not a chance," he snapped. He reached between the man's legs and gave his cock another squeeze to discourage the erection. Between his grip and cock ring, the man's penis stayed mostly flaccid. Jack continued to press against Logan's most sensitive spot until he knew the man could take no more. "Stand up."

"Thank you, Sir." He moved gingerly, his shoulders slightly hunched against the pain from the weights.

"I'm going to remove the weights but leave the ring."

"If it pleases Master."

He held the man's testicles and removed the weight with care. Logan's knees buckled again, but he whispered, "Thank you."

"Your choice, Logan. You can kneel to one side while you recover or you can assist me in beating Sinead."

Chapter Nine

Sinead's heart thundered.

She'd watched things between Jack and Logan, shocked, stunned, unable to look away. Logan's responsiveness had been elegant, something she doubted she'd ever achieve. Logan was a true submissive. She was definitely a novice with barely a toe in the water.

Jack came over to her. He crouched next to her.

Damn, with his dark hair and genuine concern in his deep blue eyes, she suddenly felt cared for. There was something about the way he looked at her, as if he could see all her secrets. "How're you doing?" he asked with his rich, deep voice.

If the devil were trying to entice a lass, he'd sound just like Jack.

Any other time, any other place, under any other circumstances, she'd have fallen for this man. If they'd met on the road and he'd introduced her to BDSM, she'd have been hooked. He was tough, unyielding, taking her where she wanted to go. He combined that with an amazing capacity for tenderness. She knew he was watching her completely, gauging her reaction.

He'd had his man clamp her nipples, and he'd encouraged Logan to apply more and more pressure before setting the clamps. There'd been safety in knowing how closely he was paying attention, looking for signs of genuine distress, but pushing when she might have otherwise said no out of fear of the unknown. With him, as closely as he kept an eye on her, she might never need to use her safe word.

She was learning to trust her nemesis.

"Sinead?"

She wanted to answer but suddenly couldn't find the words.

"Do you want to stop?"

She seriously considered her answer for a few seconds. On a scale of one to ten, she was close to a seven as far as being uncomfortable and out of her league. But there was another part of her that was turned on. Watching the interplay between the men had been erotic beyond anything she'd ever imagined.

"If you're too nervous, we can stop. Or you can utilise that uncertainty, those butterflies in your stomach, to increase the tension in this scene. Remember, you're always in control. Logan and I have played together for years. He knows his safe word and is free to use it. He's an experienced sub. We didn't start where we are. You'll progress as well. I'd never subject you to that type of beating. I don't expect that kind of response from you. It takes a while to get where Logan is. And I'll be as patient as you need."

"Sir?"

He brushed strands of hair back from her face.

That always undid her, the combination of ruthlessness and tenderness.

"Yes, little sub?"

"With all due respect... Can we damn well get on with it?"

He grinned.

Her heart did a funny little flutter in her chest.

He stood. "Right, then," he said, all business, all Dom.

He pulled his shirt over his head. His chest was a kilometre wide, and a smattering of hair trailed downward. His biceps were rippled. A very womanly part of her recognised that this man could protect her. That had never mattered to her before, but suddenly it did. What might it be like to not have to carry the load all alone?

He unfastened the button at the waist of his trousers. He wasn't wearing anything beneath the fabric. Heaven help her.

He dropped his pants and toed off his shoes, leaving them in a heap that Logan instantly gathered up.

Seeing Jack there, aroused in magnificent glory, his cock aggressively jutting towards her, she felt her pussy moisten.

"How many strokes for your impertinence, Miss?"

"Eight, Sir." That sounded like a good number...it was the same number he'd chosen for Logan's punishment.

"Ten it is. The two crimes aren't exactly the same," he continued as if reading her mind. "Logan simply moved a bit slow. You deliberately challenged my authority. Twelve or sixteen is more appropriate."

Following Logan's lead, she said, "If it pleases Sir."

"Quick learner," Logan approved.

She was terribly aware of everything from the warmth in the room to the slight discomfort of having her knees in their support, to having her wrists secured so tightly to the bench. Her arse was lewdly on display with a plug stuffed up there. Her nipples didn't hurt nearly as much as they had even a few minutes ago, probably because they were numb.

But the small discomforts seemed to heighten her arousal.

She felt rather than saw Jack move around to the rear of the bench and take the flogger from where he'd draped it across her shoulders. "I'm going to have Logan warm you up a bit," he told her. "You can trust him as much as you do me. I will be your disciplinarian, never anyone else. But since you've experienced something unusual today, I don't want to just begin your punishment. It's a mercy to be warmed up."

Her beating would be significantly more than eight blows, and that was a mercy?

Jack continued, "It will put you in the right frame of mind, bring circulation to the area so that there are fewer chances for any bruising. You'll be able to take a greater punishment. You'll crave it."

She expelled a disbelieving cough.

"Are you ready?"

She actually wasn't sure. She cleared her throat. "Yes, Sir."

"Commence, Logan. I'll let you know when she's had enough."

Involuntarily she clenched her buttocks.

"It'll go easier on you if you relax," Logan told her.

Easy for him to say.

He trailed the leather strands up the inside of her right thigh then her left. He allowed the tips to play across her lower back and her arse.

She began to move a bit, as much as the restraints would allow. She closed her eyes. Unbelievably the coldness of dread receded and was replaced with supple awareness.

The blows that landed on her thighs and arse cheeks were gentle and seductive, making something blossom inside her.

After a couple of minutes, she seemed to relax into his rhythm. The leather throngs seemed to lick at her skin in an unfulfilling tease.

She felt soothing fingers on her spine and across her shoulders. She didn't know who was touching her, and it didn't matter. Her body was tingling with desire.

She relaxed into the whip's caress and she wanted more, wanted an orgasm. She was ready to scream from the pleasure. "Thank you," she murmured, not sure if anyone heard her.

"That's a good girl," Logan said. "You're turning a lovely shade of pink. You're nearly ready for the Master's punishment, I should say."

"Indeed."

The light beating stopped. She was all but panting. Her skin was damp from perspiration while her nether region was burning from desire.

Her buttocks were being pried apart. Then she felt firmness against her pussy.

A jolt of something akin to electricity shot through her. "What...?" Oh God. Jack or maybe Logan was there, between her legs, eating out her pussy.

She was going to die and be happy to be on her way.

She was grateful to be secured so tightly to the bench. She was able to let go, to enjoy the experience, not fighting fate or herself. "May I come?" she asked.

There was no response.

She dug her fingernails into her palms as distraction. She'd learned already that no response meant no.

She tried to crawl away from the exquisite torture, but firm hands drew her back the few centimetres that she'd moved. "Please, please, please. Please may I come, Sir?"

There was no response, just harder pressure against her already swollen clit.

"Begging," she told him. "This is me begging!"

"You may come, sub."

She thrust back her hips, demanding additional pressure. Whoever was there responded, inserting a couple of fingers into her pussy and licking her hard. She screamed out her orgasm, and through her tiny drinks of oxygen, she expressed her appreciation.

"Now," Jack said, "you're ready."

Still dazed, she barely registered the first few blows. Unless she'd experienced it, she would never have believed it possible to be so saturated with pleasure that you didn't notice the pain.

"Please count."

The words registered, barely.

"I need to be sure you're with me, Sinead. Please count."

With him? She was pretty sure she wasn't. She wasn't sure where she was, but right here, right now…? No.

"That was four," Jack prompted.

"Four," she repeated dutifully.

Because her body was afire, his punishment strikes only intensified the need inside her.

He waited an interminable amount of time. "I'm ready, Sir."

He dragged out the anticipation. "Breathe," he told her.

"I'm okay."

"I want you fully in your body, fully aware."

She preferred to be floating in the ether. Even fine Irish whisky had never had this kind of effect on her.

He crouched next to her once again.

"I'll die without another orgasm," she told Jack.

He laughed. "Not likely."

"You should feel it from this side."

"Shall we continue?"

"Please," she said. And she meant it. She wanted it.

He shook out the throngs of the flogger.

Unable to resist the impulse, she kissed his hand, the one holding the flogger, the one doling out her punishment.

His brows knit together. "I'm going to fuck you until you scream, sub."

"Yes," she whispered.

He took his time moving in behind her.

"What number will this be?"

"Five," she told him, hoping she was right, but not entirely convinced.

He landed the blow.

Since there'd been a few minutes between number four and number five, she yelped. *Now* she understood what he meant about being in her body. She'd felt the nasty thud of the leather.

He landed the next on the inside of her thigh.

She cried out. The skin there was more sensitive, but exquisitely so. The pain receded quickly, leaving behind a blaze of passion. "Thank you."

The seventh landed on the inside of her other thigh. She reared up as much as the restraints would allow.

On an intellectual level, she understood more of what he'd been telling her.

Being warmed up was a mercy.

Being restrained was a blessing.

Logan had been expected to have his cock restrained and vicious weights added to his testes without struggle. The man had been expected to control his reactions whereas she was free to fight herself as much as her Dom.

"How many more, Sinead?"

She was expected to do maths? All she knew was that she needed what Jack Quinn was giving her.

"Sub?"

"However many Sir chooses." That seemed like a safe answer.

He was obviously far too clever for her. "How many have you taken?" he asked.

"Seven?"

"Is that an answer or a guess?"

"A guess," she confessed.

"Next time, no climax until after your beating is over."

She was naughty enough, horny enough, to start grinding her pelvis into the padded bench.

"Stop immediately."

As if she'd thought he wouldn't notice? "Sir, I'm coming out of my skin."

"One more. And I'll make it count. Logan, my belt if you please."

Belt?

She felt his thumb on her pussy, sliding through the moistness, pressing against her swollen nub.

"Pinch the sub's nipples."

Even though she was already wearing clamps?

In her peripheral vision, she saw Logan's movements. He fetched the belt from a hook on the wall. Seconds later she saw him again. He moved to the front of the punishment bench and squatted. He reached for her and unerringly found her already tortured nipples. He squeezed brutally. A fraction of a second later, the belt blazed across her buttocks. She cried out. The pain was torment; it was amazingly pleasurable. "Please, Sir, *fuck me.*"

Logan slowly released his grip on her nipples although he left the clamps in place.

It was seemingly forever before she felt Jack's sheathed cockhead at her entrance.

With the plug up her rear hole, his cock made her feel impossibly full. It was a wonder she could take him at all.

She wriggled back, straining against her bondage.

He took pity on her, holding her hips steady, pulling her back as he filled her cunt again and again.

"May I come?"

"No need for permission this time," he told her. "Come as often as you want."

She surrendered to her baser self. Between the plug and his engorged flesh, she was lost. He filled her completely, driving balls-deep, pulling out, thrusting in to the hilt again.

She came over and over as powerful waves of orgasms threatened to drown her.

By the time he spilled inside the condom, inside her, she was shaking, spent.

"We'll get you off the bench," he told her. "Slowly."

His voice seemed to come from a great distance.

But now that the endorphins were receding, she was aware of the pain in her nipples and the discomfort of her muscles, the itch of the plug, how swollen her pussy was and the fact she couldn't draw a complete, full breath.

Her Dom—she couldn't yet think Master—withdrew from her throbbing pussy.

"Easy," Logan coached as he released her right wrist.

At the same time, Jack released her left side. They both tended to her, rubbing her skin. Jack's hands were smooth. Logan's were work-hardened. But both men were gentle.

As if by unspoken accord, they released her knees.

She winced, becoming aware of how cramped her thighs were. It wasn't just from the restraints, she knew. It was from the way she'd unintentionally gripped the sides of the bench with her muscles, as if holding on for life.

"When you're ready, put your feet on the floor," Jack told her. "Lie there as long as you like."

She'd thought she would get up immediately, but she didn't. She was fit from all her years of dancing. But this muscular fatigue was different from anything she'd experienced before, as emotional as it was physical.

Minutes later, she moved. Logan helped her to sit up.

"I'll remove the clamps," Jack said. "There's no easy way to do this. I'll take them both off at the same time. You may want to take a deep breath before I do."

She nodded. If he gave her advice, she'd follow it. He hadn't been wrong yet.

He unclamped her nipples.

The breath she'd sucked in was expelled as she swore. "Damn it!"

"I'll let that one slide."

"You really are a beast."

"Completely." He smiled and took all the heat from the words.

Circulation returned to her nipples and the slicing pain vanished in only a second or two.

"Not so bad, was it?"

Honestly, she'd enjoyed it. Not that she'd confess that to him.

Jack uncapped a bottle of water and handed it to her. "Only a little sip," he cautioned. "Then later you can have as much as you want. Logan, fetch a robe for Sinead."

"Aye."

The man moved away.

She met Jack's gaze.

"Not because I want you covered up," he explained. "But because you'll be chilled. You've permission to shower and then join me for a whisky in front of the fire."

Maybe her brain hadn't started functioning properly because the idea of a shower and a drink sounded divine. She didn't even squabble with the idea that he'd granted permission for her to do that.

Logan returned and helped Sinead into the robe. Then Jack offered his arm as she lowered herself from the bench to the floor and tested the resiliency of her muscles.

"You did well," Jack told her.

He kissed her forehead. She could have soared. Mentally she did.

"Now I'll see to Logan. I imagine you're ready to have that cock ring removed," he said to his manservant.

"If it pleases Master."

She all but rolled her eyes. No way was she capable of that kind of submission.

Logan placed his hands behind his neck. He remained stoic as his Master handled his testicles and cock, never complaining even though it couldn't have been comfortable.

"You have two minutes to masturbate or you can save it for when you're inside Sinead. Your choice."

Logan looked at Sinead.

Impossibly she felt a tendril of desire uncurl.

Jack had hinted that the two men might take her and fill her, but the impending reality slammed her with anticipation.

"I'll wait, Sir, if it's all the same to you."

"Indeed. 'Twill be better for the waiting, I'll wager."

Belting the robe tightly around her waist, she headed for the door.

"Sinead?"

She froze and turned to look back at Jack.

"Take out the plug while you're in the shower."

She nodded.

"I don't need to remind you to leave the door open."

"No, Sir." She walked towards the bathroom, a hundred emotions churning in her. Never had she expected, at that pub in Denver, that Jack Quinn would turn her life upside down like this.

He was the answer to everything she'd always desired. Yet he was the one man she couldn't let close.

Steam billowed on top of the shower curtain, and the heat felt good on her muscles.

She stayed in the shower until the water ran cold. She was reluctant to join the men again and even more reluctant to face her internal demons.

Goosebumps rose on her skin and she turned off the water and dried off her body before she started to shiver.

Her teeth all but chattered as she wrapped herself in the oversized robe.

She heard the murmur of voices. Despite herself, she was drawn into the living room, towards Jack.

A strong wind blew off Clew Bay. The windows rattled with the howl. Under other circumstances, she might have said the sound was the Banshee.

Rain threatened.

Jack was stoking the flames. And when he heard her, he looked up. "You're beautiful, Sinead."

She flushed. She'd never been called more than pretty. But there was no lie in his eyes or his voice. To him, maybe she was beautiful.

While she'd showered, a plate of meats and cheese had been put up, probably by Logan. The man was handy to have around.

"Whisky?" Jack offered.

He poured three drinks. He offered one to her, another to Logan, then took one for himself. For a moment she could almost believe this scene was normal. Logan was dressed once again in trousers and a dark sweater. A black T-shirt snuggled Jack's broad shoulders, and dark slacks hung perfectly on him, as if custom tailored, which, she realised, they probably had been.

It could have been a normal country scene except for the fact she was wearing a robe and her arse was reddened from a flogger. And if Jack commanded either her or Logan to their knees to suck his penis, they would.

She accepted a small glass and tossed it back in a single gulp.

"Easy, lass."

Her nerves slightly settled, she picked at a few pieces of cheese.

Within a few minutes, rain lashed the house, suiting her mood. Pent up feelings clawed at her, and she had no idea what to do with them. She needed to get away, and in this weather, she never would.

He poured her a second drink. It went down as smoothly as the first.

"Sit," he told her. "We'll talk."

"I'll be in the kitchen," Logan said.

He took a seat in one of the chairs near the fire, legs outstretched and crossed at the ankles. "You look as if you're ready for battle, much like your ancestor, Bridget," he told her. "Who are you fighting, Sinead? Me? Or yourself?"

She wished she could answer that.

"If you were to set aside the fight, for now, what would you do?"

She sank into the other chair.

"With the weather, we're stuck here with each other." He rolled his glass between his palms. "Tell me you hated it."

"You know I didn't." The whisky warmed her from the inside out. "But that's what I hate."

"Is it the submission you dislike? Or is it me you despise?"

She looked at him squarely. "You."

He nodded, seemingly not offended in the least. "We're good at the submission and Dominance?"

She nodded reluctantly.

"Yet you hate me for being the same man who you want to dominate you."

She stood and paced in front of the fire. "I don't like being bossed around, Jack." Outside of a scene, she refused to call him Sir. Leave that to his manservant. "I don't like you showing up uninvited in my life and demanding I marry you. I have my own life, things I like to do. Touring. My drums. My dancing. My music. My passions." She remembered how Donal wanted her to grow up and quit playing, be a wife and mother.

He nodded. "What else?"

"I don't believe in curses, but I do believe in bad blood between our clans. We can be friends, let bygones be bygones. I'll shake your hand, you can shake mine."

"Marriage between us makes perfect sense," he said steadily. "Curse or no, joining our family holdings makes sense. Your family is struggling needlessly. The lands are fertile and rich, and we can cultivate them." He paused, looked at her, then continued, "You're single. So am I. Children will cement the future for the family holdings. From a business standpoint it makes perfect sense. People have done this since the beginning of time."

He was right about that. But she was to sacrifice herself for a *business* decision?

"We're compatible sexually, or we will be once you learn a few more manners."

She stopped her pacing at stared at him, aghast.

"That was a joke, wombat. Nothing more."

"I won't give up who I am, Jack."

"Every business decision has negotiation."

"I won't negotiate."

"Come here, lass."

When he got that husky note in his voice, she was helpless to resist. She put her empty glass on the mantelpiece while he slid his onto an end table. She crossed to him. She wouldn't marry him, but she couldn't resist the tug of his sexual allure.

He grabbed her upper arms and dragged her on top of him, her knees on either side of his hips.

He was all man, muscled and tight. Their gazes met, locked. "I'm going to kiss you."

Kiss?

It was one thing to fuck, another entirely to be intimate.

He claimed her mouth, and she tasted the burn of the alcohol. He intoxicated her. He gently met her tongue. He coaxed and tested rather than dominated.

Undone, she responded.

In him she'd met her match. He wasn't intimidated by her. He knew how to read her. He knew what she wanted.

Emboldened, she dug her fingers into his dark hair, the locks curled from the humidity. A fine specimen, if she did say so. There could be worse things than bedding this Irishman.

His hand was on her cunt. Instead of pulling back, she leaned into him. She thrust her tongue into his mouth.

He stroked her clit, then teased it a bit harder. Even though he'd wrung multiple climaxes from her, she was on the edge again. "Jack, Sir—"

"Don't," he warned softly. "Don't come."

"But—"

"Fight it. Ride it."

Her breaths were short little bursts.

"Not yet."

"Then, don't...dinna d—" She moaned. "You'll have to...stop..." She was there, almost there, ready to explode—

"Take it. Take everything I offer."

She rode his hand, grinding herself against him. She couldn't believe she was doing this. Since she'd met him, she'd clearly lost her mind. Clearly, totally, without question lost her mind.

"Come for me, Sinead."

With a whimper, she shattered.

"You're one hot woman," he told her.

"There's something about you…"

"About us," he corrected. "Takes two."

"Damn you, Jack."

"Someday, you'll remember to call me Sir." He nipped her ear. "And one day, you'll call me Master."

Ordinarily she'd take that bet. But if he insisted on being called Master before he allowed her to come, she was afraid he'd win.

Chapter Ten

The music, she knew well. She should. She'd written the tune.

She blinked, bringing the world into awareness. She felt disoriented in the big bed, all alone. Having a man in her bed was unusual, so why did the absence of him feel strange, rather than comfortable?

It all returned in a series of snapshots.

Jack Quinn.

The island.

The beating.

Their time together.

Her exhaustion, mental and physical. She had a vague memory of him kissing her, giving her an orgasm then carrying her to bed.

The last few days, since she'd taken the stage in Denver, had been dizzying. A hurried transatlantic flight, meeting his grandmother, being bound and beaten, then stolen away to an uninhabited island, so close to the mainland, so close and an eternity away felt surreal, like stepping into an Andy Warhol painting. She was herself, who she'd always been, and yet she felt entirely different, as if she'd never again be the same.

Jack Quinn.

Hated enemy.

Lover.

She was losing her mind.

She still heard the pipes. That, at least, hadn't been part of a dream.

This piece was sorrowful, the bagpipes mourning. It had a haunting melody that she hoped reminded people of Eire. She wanted the music to linger and tease. Much like the man she'd been thinking of when she'd composed it…a man she hadn't known at the time, the man who now dominated her waking and sleeping hours.

The faint sound of bagpipes lured her from the covers.

Wrapping the ridiculously large robe over her naked body—of course he hadn't allowed her to sleep in any clothes—she followed the siren's song towards the front of the house.

She saw him in the living room, looking out the window, his back to her. Dusk was gathering. The rain had eased, but it hadn't ceased.

He had her music playing on a CD.

He stared into the distance, probably seeing, as she was, the outline of Croagh Logan. What was he thinking? Of the future? Of his duties and responsibilities?

She was thinking of earlier, with him, with Logan. Memories filled her, making her pussy tingle.

Seeming to sense her presence, he turned.

"Home," she whispered, looking into the distance.

"Aye. Yours and mine, Sinead."

"Unforgivable, what our ancestors did to one another."

"Castle Cairn had been in my family long years afore all this started. As my grandmother discussed, our fortunes have been seemingly linked. We lost Castle Cairn. According to history, it was a square tower castle, with stone walls and a moat. It was commanding in its day. Must have been formidable for the O'Malleys to even consider approaching. There's not much left of it now. A lone pillar remains."

"I've heard stones from the castle were used in some of the oldest buildings in Westport."

"Could be true. We used some of the stones in re-building. And what of your home, Sinead?"

"Like you, we rebuilt from the ashes. We've held on through the years. I've turned our home into a bed-and-breakfast, *Radharc Na Mara* Manor, to help it pay its keep. I've added self-catering cottages." She shrugged. "It's a living."

"Seaside Manor," he translated, the words sexy on his tongue. "Ireland's worth it, isn't she? Any sacrifice, anything to hold onto the land, the history."

A mist rolled in from the sea. "She's worth it," Sinead agreed.

"It seems both our families lost."

"You've an interesting idea of what lost means, Quinn. Your home is still beautiful," she said.

"Aye. We're proud of our heritage, the greenhouses, the sheep we continue to raise, the linens we produce."

"Not so bad, that."

"Unless there's no one to bequeath it to. A millennium of struggle for...what? Do you wonder? If you have no children, what will happen to your family's remaining lands?"

"There are cousins."

He propped a hip on the window sill. "You'll struggle and sacrifice for others to inherit?"

She shrugged. "That's the way of it. What of you, Jack?"

"I will have children."

She had a sudden image of him with a smiling wife and adoring children. Her jaw tightened. She didn't want him. Why should she care if someone else did?

"And the woman you were with?"

"Maeve? Beautiful as a sunrise. Unfaithful as a cur." He folded his arms across his chest. "After I found out, we argued. She ran away from me."

She winced. His words were unemotional, but she sensed the anguish behind them. And no wonder he had such issues when she fled. "I'm sorry for your loss."

"It's history."

"Is it?"

"I lost Maeve and the future I thought we were going to have. But I'll not lose my future and I will see my grandmother's mind at ease."

His voice was tight. This man was deeper than the North Sea. She'd seen him as single minded and determined in a way that made him nothing more than a pain in her rear. She understood him better now, his commitment. The way he loved his grandmother was remarkable.

"What of you, Sinead?"

"There's nothing to say, honestly. I was nearly engaged. But he wanted to control me, babies and boring sex. He wanted me to give up my music, my dancing, even composing."

"That would have been a loss."

She shook her head. "It couldn't have happened. My music is part of me. I couldn't give it up. It'd be like

204

cutting out a piece of my soul. I cannot give up who I am for anyone else. I learned that the hard way."

"I wouldn't ask you to give up your music."

"I love to tour. There's no way you'd allow your wife to be on tour for months at a time."

He didn't respond.

Allowing her to compose was one thing, allowing her to fly off was another. "And what if we had children, what then? You and I, we've reached an impasse, Jack. When the weather clears, you'll be wanting to take me back to the mainland."

"We'll be seeing about that, lass."

"No matter how many times you ask, the answer will be 'no'."

* * * *

Jack was not going to play fair.

He was going to spend the rest of his life with this woman. He wanted her bound to him, but he wasn't a fool. A marriage certificate, ring, vows, meant little. They lacked the substance he demanded. He wanted her so tied to him by the time they left the island that she'd be powerless to walk away from him or his grandmother's wish.

She was right that her career would cause problems, but there was nothing they couldn't work out. The challenge would be in convincing her.

He planned to use the remaining time to pleasure Sinead in ways she'd never imagined. The man she'd nearly married had provided boring sex, in her words. Jack sure as hell could do better than that. "Back to the bedroom."

Her beautiful eyes widened. "Did you hear a word I said?"

"Do you see the fog rolling in? We're going nowhere until tomorrow. I've no intention of playing checkers while I could be fucking you."

She parted her mouth.

"It's your choice. Walk or crawl."

"Your way or your way?" she challenged.

He changed his tone, making it rough and commanding. "Move, sub, or I'll have you over my knee."

She lowered her gaze.

The moment he'd taken that tone, she'd responded. How could she not see how perfect she was for him? "I've changed my mind. Drop that robe this instant and crawl."

Still keeping her gaze downcast, she unbelted the robe and shrugged off the material.

Without him prompting her a second time, she lowered herself to the floor and crawled to the bedroom.

"On all fours on the bed," he told her.

Her motions were undeniably graceful. She was a fast learner. "I've decided not to wait for Logan's return," he told her. "I'll be the first one to have you up the arse."

"I'm not sure I'm ready for you to take me up the—"

"I don't recall offering you a choice." He noticed her breaths were shallow. From fear? "You've had a plug up there. That'll help, but we'll still need patience." He stripped off his clothes and tossed them on the end of the bed.

He tore a condom free from its packet and sheathed himself in it. After he squirted lube onto his hand, he teased her clit. Then he spread the lube down the length of his hard, throbbing cock. He wanted her so badly, his balls were swollen with need. "You're so wet."

"We could just do this traditionally, like regular missionary sex."

"We could," he agreed. "But we're not going to. No boring sex here, Sinead." He placed the tip of his cock at the entrance to her tightest hole and pushed just a little before backing off again. "You're lubed. You've been stretched. You're ready."

"Jack—"

"Sir," he corrected, with a sharp slap to her right flank.

She nodded slightly.

He moved in behind her again and pressed his cockhead against her hole.

She jerked way from him.

He swatted her ass, pinched her clit, fucked her pussy with two fingers then told her, "Keep still."

"I'll try," she promised.

He imprisoned her hips. "Remember to breathe."

"It—"

Her word was lost as he bore down. "Breathe," he instructed. Damn. But he had no idea how much more restraint he could show. He needed to be in her, needed to feel his balls slap her pussy as he impaled her.

He yanked back on her hips as he surged forward with his dick. With a final, hard push, he was there. He exhaled a shaky breath of his own. Taking an anal virgin was total satisfaction. "We're there."

"I can't do this! We need to stop. You need to get out of me!"

"We're there," he said again. "Be still a moment."

"It burns."

"*Muirnín*," he murmured. "Be still." He fisted his hand in her hair, then skimmed his touch lightly across her back.

He felt her relax and open up. "That's it. That's my girl." He began to pump in her. Soon, he felt her answering movements. 'Twouldn't take long for his climax to overtake him.

He concentrated on her, servicing her clit, whispering endearments, feeling her orgasm build.

His balls were near to exploding when she began to pant. "Come," he told her, "come now."

When she shuddered and wriggled, she drove him over the cliff. Grabbing hold of her shoulders instead of her hips, he kept her captive as he drained his balls into her hole.

He held her for a few moments, because he could. Then, after he pulled out, he cradled her with the protective tenderness she deserved.

His woman.

His woman.

She'd know it soon enough.

Logan called out a greeting as he returned to the cottage.

There was a caretaker's cottage a small distance away where Logan lived. The man had excused himself to cook their evening meal. He hadn't wanted to disturb Sinead, and he preferred cooking in his own kitchen. As he'd often said, his knives were far better than the ones Jack kept in his cottage.

Sinead excused herself to clean up while Logan set the table and Jack uncorked a bottle of wine to complement Logan's speciality — lamb curry.

She joined them, damp tendrils of hair curled at her nape. She donned another cheeky T-shirt, one about so many men, so little time. But she'd worn a skirt.

"Bend over so I can see you're bare beneath."

She bent and saucily flipped up her skirt and let him drink his fill before taking her seat.

Lord, she would be the death of him.

Jack enjoyed the meal, one sub seated to his right, the other to his left. He could see his future like this...the vixen fighting him at every turn, his manservant providing comfort.

After Logan and Sinead had tidied up, refusing his offer of help, they joined him in the living room. Jack refreshed the wine, draining the bottle.

"Sinead wishes to return to the mainland tomorrow," he told Logan. "So we've got tonight."

"Aye, Sir."

"Wait..." she said. But even as she protested, her cheeks flushed red. "Both of you? I didn't really know you were serious."

"You know your safe word."

"'Tisn't seemly."

"No," he agreed. "Nor is it boring. Now take off your clothes." Jack looked at Logan. "Both of you."

He fed the fire while his submissives dutifully removed their clothing.

Both stood with their backs to the fire waiting his command. There wasn't a more lovely sight. Two beautiful humans, one rugged and hard, the other feminine and soft, waiting for his pleasure. "We'll go in the bedroom," he said. "Logan, fetch a pair of tweezer clamps for Sinead. I believe we have lubricant from earlier."

"Aye, Sir."

Jack followed Sinead into the bedroom. "Kneel up." He knew she found comfort in his commands, it allowed her a respite from arguing and from thinking. Who was he fooling? It allowed him a respite, as well.

Logan entered almost immediately with the clamps.

"These are lightweight," he told Sinead. "Your nipples are already sensitive, so you don't need anything too intense. But this will just add a little extra pleasure." He gently squeezed her nipples and she moaned quietly. "You're so responsive. Any man who won't give you what you want and desire is a fool." He affixed the clamps and she wavered a bit. "You're all right?"

She nodded. "Just near an orgasm again, Sir."

He smelt her arousal and wanted her again. "Logan, on the bed."

The man pulled back the bedcovers and lay on his back.

"Take him in your mouth, Sinead."

Sinead crawled up onto the bed and sucked Logan into her mouth. His own cock hardened just from the sight. When the man was hard, Jack put his hand in her hair and eased her away.

He grabbed a couple of condoms from the nightstand. He gave one to her. "Put it on Logan."

Her hands shook a bit as she opened the package and pulled out the condom. "I've never done this before," she confessed.

"I'll be patient," Logan promised.

Jack shucked his clothes while she rolled the condom down the man's length.

Finally, she looked up at him. "Lower yourself on him," he instructed. "Assuming you're lubricated enough?"

She laughed a little tightly. "I'm wet, Sir."

"Good." He joined them on the bed. He held her around the waist while she lowered herself onto Logan's throbbing cock.

Then he knelt, knees wide, above Logan's head so she could suck him hard, as well.

She lowered her head towards his cock without being told and lapped up the pre-ejaculate.

"Ride him," he told Sinead. "But do not come, either of you. Logan. If you need a cock ring, just ask. I'll go easy on the punishment for the favour."

"Indeed I will, Sir."

He closed his eyes for a few seconds while she gave him a blowjob. A lot of women didn't get the right amount of pressure, right there, beneath the head, but she did. And she used her hand perfectly as well.

If she thought he was ever letting her go, she was mistaken.

When he was good and hard, he took her head between his palms and moved her away. "It wouldn't do for me to spill my load when I told Logan he couldn't come, now, would it?"

"I do like sucking you, though, Sir." She licked her upper lip for emphasis.

"Sheathe me, sub." He grabbed a condom from the sheet and handed it to her.

"Having you there makes me want to suck your balls, Sir," Logan said.

"Easy," Jack cautioned. "I'm only human."

After she sheathed him—and wasn't her grip sure and sexy?—she smiled shyly.

"You've had me up your arse," he told her. "But it will be different with both of us."

She nodded.

"Are you ready?"

"Yes," she whispered.

Chapter Eleven

She was unable to believe this was happening. She was with two men, one of them filling her pussy, keeping her on the knife edge of sensual fulfilment.

Logan's penis was beautiful. While it wasn't a long as Jack's, it was thick and heavily veined. She rode him, mindful of Jack's orders that neither of them come.

Jack moved behind her. She felt his finger seeking entrance to her tightest hole. He was right, this was different. Already being full made the other seem nearly impossible.

Jack seemed to reach the same realisation.

"Sinead, get off Logan. Logan, keep your cock hard."

He positioned Sinead on all fours. She reached for Logan's cock, placing her hand on his, stroking him.

Relentlessly, despite her mewls of protest, he continued to enter a little, pull back, then start again, going deeper each time.

Logan reached up and fingered her pussy. "Yes! Thank you. She needed that, needed the distraction and pleasure.

"Almost there," Jack told her, his hands on her shoulders. "Almost there." He thrust forward.

She screamed and lost her balance, but Logan was there to catch her, to continue to tease her, despite her death grip on his shaft.

"Good girl," Jack approved.

His approval was all she needed to completely relax.

"Let me inside you," Logan said.

Which meant, in other words, let go of his cock.

With Jack's guidance, she maneuvered her body into place.

"Slowly," Jack urged.

With her Dom filling her rear, she slid down Logan's length. She was breathless, ragged. Two men inside her both filling and stretching her.

Perspiration dotted her body.

She wasn't sure she could do this. Every muscle tensed and her breathing became a bit irregular.

"Let go, *Muirnín.*"

"Finger your pussy," Logan urged.

She did, allowing the men to support her.

Then it was as if magic happened. She stopped fighting herself. She surrendered to the sensations. Climax after climax claimed her as her body was stretched and tormented and pleased. She felt hands on her everywhere, supporting her, teasing her. She'd never imagined anything like this could exist.

"You may come at any time, Logan," Jack said, as if from a great distance.

She felt the explosion of Logan's climax, his pulsing, his shudder. The sheer physicalness of it made her come again.

Jack held her firmly then he thrust up inside her high and deep and grunting as he climaxed.

She was spent.

She collapsed on top of Logan; he stroked her hair, soothing her, complimenting her.

She was hardly aware of the men moving around, changing positions, but she realised she was on her side with a cold cloth placed against her entire private area.

She dozed, and when she woke, she was in her Dom's arms. Weak moonlight hit the window, and he pulled her against him.

"I'm not letting you go."

For the first time, she didn't protest. In this moment, she didn't want him to let her go.

Dawn was streaming through the window when her mobile rang. She was tempted to ignore it, but she wasn't wired that way.

Blinking herself awake, she tossed back the sheets and headed for the living room.

Jack followed her, wrapping the robe around her shoulders.

She checked the caller identification screen. "It's My cousin, Mary." She cleared her throat and answered.

"Sin, sorry to bother you."

"You're never a bother." She realised Mary probably thought she was still in the States. "You can call me any time." She snuggled into the robe and Jack's silent support. "What's going on?"

"You'll think I'm a ninny. And I wouldn't have called unless, well, unless you called the other day."

"You're not a ninny." Mary was never one for overreaction. She was the steady one in the family, the least prone to flights of fancy.

Jack moved off, towards the kitchen and, hopefully, coffee.

"Well, I found a silver comb. Or rather, your ma did. She didn't want me to tell you."

She sank onto the settee.

She might not believe in curses, but she wasn't one for coincidence either. "I'll be home soon," she promised.

"Your ma will have my head for telling you."

"She won't know," Sinead promised. "Your secret is safe with me." After a couple of minutes of chitchat, they rang off.

She put the robe on properly and wrapped up in it.

Jack brought her a cup of coffee, heavy on the cream.

"I'll marry you," she said, accepting the cup and taking a sip. Not only had he got the cream exact, he'd also added enough sugar. She couldn't fault the way he tried. She could only fault that she had to go through with this. "If you'll have me."

He crouched in front of her. He was all man. Well, that wasn't the total truth of it. He was all Dom.

"What's happened?"

She felt numb. "My mother found a comb." She took a sip of the coffee and shook back her hair. "It probably means nothing, but I can't continue like this. I found one. Your grandmother found one. There was one in Maeve's car, in your mother's car. If there's any chance my sacrifice can make a difference, I will do it."

"Marrying me would be a sacrifice, would it?"

His eyes registered the shock of hurt.

"I'm sorry. That was thoughtless. I didn't mean it to sound that way."

"Be certain of what you're saying, lass. If you marry me, there will never be a divorce. I'll fight you through hell and back."

"I understand."

He took the cup from her. "Not exactly the way I'd imagined this happening."

"I'm a modern woman." She forced a small smile.

"I'm not a modern man, I'm afraid. We'll sort it out. But be very clear on this. You'll marry me, Sinead?"

As if there had ever been a choice. Eight hundred years had led to this moment. Every event, every decision, every twist of fate. She didn't feel jubilant. She felt trapped.

* * * *

"Do you need to be spanked?" Jack asked.

She'd learned a one-finger response in America. Right now, she was sorely tempted to use it.

"Maybe I should lick your cunt? You're much more compliant after that."

He took her breath away.

He stood in the entrance to his suite at his grandmother's house, a broad shoulder braced against the jamb. He wore a dark suit that made his eyes even more staggeringly blue, like a sunrise over a cold mountain peak. He was devastatingly handsome. "The priest is waiting."

They were to marry today—in fact, it should have happened already. Jack had moved quickly when she'd agreed to marry him. He'd had the agreement drawn up in less than twenty-four hours. He'd taken her shopping, bought her a dress, all before the sun set again. He'd summoned the priest immediately. He'd offered to invite her family, but she knew they'd try to talk her out of it. "I'm hurrying," she said. Because she was frustrated, because her hands shook, she'd already stabbed a fingernail through a pair of silken stockings. This second pair was in danger, too. Since when did she, a woman who preferred bare legs and T-shirts, shimmy into beautiful lingerie?

He came into the room, gently closing the door behind him. "Is it so bad?" he asked. "The idea of marrying me?"

"Yes." She looked away. "No."

"Sulking doesn't look good on you, my warrior." He pulled her up off the bed. "You're lovely, Sinead."

She laughed. "I've got one blasted stocking attached to this stupid garter, and I don't know whether the knickers go over the garter belt or under. And this bra. Lord take me. My nipples are bare." She shook her head. Then emotion crashed into her in a powerful whoosh. "What the hell am I doing, Jack?"

"Thinking too much." He pulled her against him then he shocked the breath from her lungs when he tossed her on the bed.

He sat on the edge of the mattress, and reached for her, dragging her across his knee.

"What in the hell do you think you're doing?"

He swatted her bare butt, hard.

She yelped. "Stop it, this instant."

He spanked her again. And again. And again.

She was gasping, stunned, unable to think.

Then he yanked his belt from its loops and laid leather against her skin.

She muffled her scream.

Sierra Cartwright

"Thank me, sub. Thank me for beating you."

He continued to spank her mercilessly.

Gulping in great gasps of air, she managed a whispered thank you. Then another. Somewhere along the line she lost track of his blows and her shouts of gratitude.

"Spread your legs."

Helpless to resist him, not wanting to resist him, she did.

Ruthlessly he parted her labia. In less than thirty seconds, he brought her to a shuddering climax.

She hadn't started to think again when she felt something hard trying to intrude in her tightest hole. "What...?"

"A butt plug," he told her.

"I'm not wearing a butt plug to my wedding!"

"You don't have a choice." He held her captive with one arm, tightening his grip the more she wiggled. With his other hand, he squirted lube onto the plug. At least, please, please, please, let that be what he was doing.

He opened her anus, stretching it wide with three fingers before starting to work on the plug. "Where is this going?" he asked.

"You're going to hell," she said.

He tutted. "I'll ask again." He slid the plug back and forth, twisting it to work it in deeper. "Where is this plug going?"

He knew her, knew her too well, knew her responses, knew what she wanted. She was wild and wanton, needed his touch.

"Tell me, Sinead."

"My arse." The words were more panted than spoken. "It's going in my arse. Please." He gave a final push. "Agh!"

"Beautiful," he said. Then he pushed her from his lap. "Stand up. And then bend over, grabbing your ankles."

Her head spun, but she blindly followed orders.

"It's a glass plug," he told her. "Meaning I can see into your ass. Think about that as you promise to love, honour and obey." He pulled on the plug, then shoved it in again.

It was so deep, she was so full.

"It looks sexy. I'll barely be able to get through the vows, thinking about your arse being stretched wide for me."

"Jack…"

He helped her to stand erect, then took her in his arms, kissing her. She closed her eyes. Wishing… If he loved her, her dreams would be coming true. Instead, it was little more than a business agreement.

Rather than watch her struggle, he helped her with her stockings, fastening them in place with the garter belt. He suckled on her exposed nipples. "Maybe we should skip the wedding and go straight to the honeymoon."

"I thought we already had." Unbelievably, she was wet, soaked, and from more than just the lube he'd used. Despite their problems, they had this in common. He was everything she needed — wanted — in a man.

He held the gown for her while she shimmied into it.

He smoothed her hair into place. "I'm honoured you'll be my bride."

"I'm a dishevelled mess."

"You're breathtaking. You look like a woman who's been fucked. There is nothing sexier." He reached into his pocket. "I have a wedding gift for you." He shrugged. "Not much, but it's a token."

Her heart swelled. If she were a weepy woman, she'd be a watering pot right now. The golden pendant on a chain bore a picture of Saint Patrick.

"When we're apart, I hope it provides protection."

"Thank you," she whispered, lifting her hair so he could fasten the gift in place.

"Now, wombat, are you ready to get married, or do you need another spanking?"

"One is sufficient."

"How does the plug feel?" he asked, as he guided her down the stairs.

"Awkward. Uncomfortable. Full."

He smiled. "In other words, perfect?"

She couldn't believe how he'd settled her down, calmed her fears, restored everything to rights.

Catherine had thought of a bouquet, and she'd added sprigs of four-leaf clover to it for luck.

For the music, Jack had selected a piece she'd composed.

The ceremony was quick, thankfully, because she wasn't sure how much longer she could tolerate the plug.

And afterward, as Jack offered a toast to his bride, Catherine smiled and offered her own wishes. "To many healthy children, to happiness, to the end of the curse."

Logan lifted his glass in their direction. His knowing smile told her he intended to be part of the honeymoon. She shivered with anticipation. Things could be worse.

"I'm glad you two love one another."

"Love?" Sinead asked.

"*Máthair Chríona?*"

Catherine frowned. "You do love one another, right? You chose him."

Oh God.

"The curse is specific. There has to be love."

"Love?" Sinead demanded. "You never told us that." She looked at Jack. "I'm sorry. I don't love you. I can't love a man who doesn't love me." Tears streamed down her face.

Catherine looked stricken.

Sinead dropped her flowers as she ran out the door.

Chapter Twelve

Nothing like work to soothe the savage beast that was her soul.

Over the last five days, she'd composed a new tune. One could be guaranteed it wouldn't be played at weddings and birthdays. More like funerals and for those on suicide watch.

She'd returned home to *Radharc Na Mara* Manor, to lick her wounds. She hurt. She ached. She was lonely. She wanted Jack. She wanted...

Love.

Right.

As if he was capable of it.

He was all about duty, nothing else.

She blinked back tears. Sinead O'Malley did not cry over men. She didn't, she didn't—

Even if her heart was broken. Even if she...

Loved him?

That wasn't possible.

She'd sworn never to love again after Donal. In fact, she didn't even believe in it. It was a wild emotion that opened you to be battered and bruised. She couldn't love; she would have to give up who she was. But there it was. She was battered and bruised.

Why else was she working like a madwoman?

For truth, she'd missed the manor, its hustle and bustle, its eccentric guests. The Major and his newest wife were back again. Well, the Major was back again. This was the first visit for wife number seven. Lord love him. Sinead wasn't willing to do it properly even once.

But she was working round the clock so she didn't have to think. Didn't have to see his face every time she closed her eyes. Didn't have to curl into a lonely ball in the big, oversized bed.

She swiped her knuckles across her eyes and was refreshing beverages in the breakfast room when the front door blew open and slammed against the back wall.

"Yum and chocolate in one tight package... Who's that delicious morsel?"

At her cousin's words, Sinead looked up.

'Twasn't the wind that blew the door open, 'twas Jack who slammed it open.

"I'm Jack Quinn," he told Mary.

"The Jack Quinn?" She made the sign of the cross.

"Sinead's husband."

Sinead's heart leapt into her throat and threatened to choke her.

"Sinead's —" Mary broke off. She looked at Sinead then Jack.

"Husband," he repeated.

The Major and his wife stopped eating and stared at the pair. The Major's fork was paused in the air, a piece of ham attached.

"Not here and not now," Sinead pleaded.

"'Tis true," Mary demanded. "You've married a Quinn?"

"You need to leave," Sinead said, wishing her voice sounded stronger, wishing she had the courage of her words. In truth, all she wanted to do was touch him, kiss him, feel the power of his possession.

"Not without my wife."

"We didn't—" Because they hadn't consummated their wedding, their marriage could be annulled, right? She put down the tea pot before she dropped it.

"Here and now." He was unyielding. "Unless you want a public spectacle, you'll see me in your office."

"You've married a Quinn?" Mary asked. "God help us all."

How in the hell would she explain this?

With his fingertips pressed to the small of her back, he urged her towards the privacy of her office.

The door hadn't closed behind them when he crushed her lips beneath his.

His kiss was searing. And it tasted different. It tasted of…desperation?

She pulled back, confused.

"Damn it," he said, stepping away and dragging a hand through his hair. "Enough is enough. I want you in my life. I want you in my bed. I want you under me, screaming my name as I fuck you ragged." He drew a breath. Before she could say anything, he continued, "I've totally gone and done it."

"Done it?"

"Damn it. Fallen in love with you. Never intended to. Never wanted to. But there it is. This isn't about the damnable curse. It's not about my *máthair Chríona*. It's about you. Wombat. Vixen."

"You love me?"

"Crazy, stupid. Head over heels. Can't live without you." He paced, formed his hands into fists. Nervousness?

She was speechless. Her heart thundered. Her mouth dropped open.

"Tell me you love me. Or tell me I'm a fool. If you make me go away, I will."

The tears she'd been denying flooded her eyes. Sinead launched herself into his arms, wrapping her legs around his waist. She nipped his ear and dug her hands into his hair. She kissed him senseless, her overpowering, powerful and humbled man.

"Tell me," he demanded. "But before you do, know this... I will not settle for anything less than your total commitment, emotionally and physically. Everything you have to offer, I want. And more. There will be no half-measures between us."

"I love you, you oaf! I've loved you since the island." He was everything she'd ever wanted, dreamt of, fantasised about. "I can't live without you."

"*Bean mo chroi*," he murmured. *Woman of my heart*. I am not pleased about the idea of you being on the road after we have children, but I'll manage. You may need to soothe the savage beast that is your spouse, but I'll not stand between you and your dreams."

She threw her arms around his neck.

He disentangled her. "About that honeymoon..." He locked the door. "Show me your cunt."

Her nerves jumped into her stomach. She gulped, then complied, dropping her trousers and knickers.

"I'm going to take you, Sinead. Here. Now. Fast. Hard. I will prove you belong to me. Bend over. Legs apart."

She trembled, knowing what to expect.

The first stroke was a feathered touch. That was unexpected. The second was a light slap. That was more or less what she expected.

The third was a stinging slap that ignited her pussy.

She would have collapsed, but he caught her. "Tell me," he urged.

"You're everything I've always wanted." He'd been right all that time ago when he'd told her she'd lacked the courage to face herself, her feelings, her wants, her desire, her passion. Now, she'd found it. "Fuck me, Jack." She stood, faced him, unzipped his pants. "Here. Now." She planted her hands on the desk, bending over.

She felt his cock against her. She moved back, demandingly.

"My woman."

"My man. My Master."

About the Author

Born in Northern England and raised in the Wild West, Sierra Cartwright pens book that are as untamed as the Rockies she calls home.

She's an award-winning, multi-published writer who wrote her first book at age nine and hasn't stopped since.

Sierra invites you to share the complex journey of love and desire, of surrender and commitment. Her own journey has taught her that trusting takes guts and courage, and her work is a celebration for everyone who is willing to take that risk.

Sierra Cartwright loves to hear from readers.

You can find her contact information, website details and author profile page at http://www.total-e-bound.com

Total-E-Bound Publishing

www.total-e-bound.com

Take a look at our exciting range of literagasmic™
erotic romance titles and discover pure quality
at Total-E-Bound.

Lightning Source UK Ltd.
Milton Keynes UK
UKOW052148180612

194657UK00001B/100/P